SCOUT PRESS

Dear Reader,

You are about to begin one of the most unnerving, chilling, philosophical, and page-turning novels of the past decade. And yes, I stand by that claim.

In Iain Reid's masterful debut, two people are going on a long car ride to a distant farm. The driver's name is Jake, and his passenger is known only as "the girlfriend." When a minor snowfall escalates into a menacing blizzard, they are forced to pull off the road. To tell you anything more about the plot would ruin the reading experience—and trust me, it is an "experience."

What I will tell you is this: you will be terrified.

But you will have absolutely no idea why . . .

Keep the lights on.

Yours,

Alison Callahan
Executive Editor
Scout Press
Alison.Callahan@simonandschuster.com

www.simonandschuster.com
A CBS COMPANY

I'M THINKING OF ENDING THINGS

Iain Reid

SCOUT PRESS

New York   London   Toronto   Sydney   New Delhi

Scout Press
An Imprint of Simon & Schuster, Inc.
1230 Avenue of the Americas
New York, NY 10020

First Scout Press hardcover edition June 2016

SCOUT PRESS and colophon are registered trademarks of Simon & Schuster, Inc.

For information about special discounts for bulk purchases, please contact Simon & Schuster Special Sales at 1-866-506-1949 or business@simonandschuster.com.

The Simon & Schuster Speakers Bureau can bring authors to your live event. For more information or to book an event, contact the Simon & Schuster Speakers Bureau at 1-866-248-3049 or visit our website at www.simonspeakers.com.

Interior design by Jaime Putorti

Manufactured in the United States of America

10 9 8 7 6 5 4 3 2 1

Library of Congress Cataloging-in-Publication Data is available.

ISBN 978-1-5011-2692-5
ISBN 978-1-5011-2696-3 (ebook)

To Don Reid

I'M THINKING OF ENDING THINGS

I'm thinking of ending things.

Once this thought arrives, it stays. It sticks. It lingers. It dominates. There's not much I can do about it. Trust me. It doesn't go away. It's there whether I like it or not. It's there when I eat. When I go to bed. It's there when I sleep. It's there when I wake up. It's always there. Always.

I haven't been thinking about it for long. The idea is new. But it feels old at the same time. When did it start? What if this thought wasn't conceived by me but planted in my mind, predeveloped? Is an unspoken idea unoriginal? Maybe I've actually known all along. Maybe this is how it was always going to end.

Jake once said, "Sometimes a thought is closer to truth, to reality, than an action. You can say anything, you can do anything, but you can't fake a thought."

You can't fake a thought. And this is what I'm thinking.

It worries me. It really does. Maybe I should have known how it was going to end for us. Maybe the end was written right from the beginning.

T
he road is mostly empty. It's quiet around here. Vacant. More so than anticipated. So much to see but not many people, not many buildings or houses. Sky. Trees. Fields. Fences. The road and its gravel shoulders.

"You want to stop for a coffee?"

"I think I'm okay," I say.

"Last chance we'll have before it becomes really farmy."

I'm visiting Jake's parents for the first time. Or I will be when we arrive. Jake. My boyfriend. He hasn't been my boyfriend for very long. It's our first trip together, our first long drive, so it's weird that I'm feeling nostalgic—about our relationship, about him, about us. I should be excited, looking forward to the first of many. But I'm not. Not at all.

"No coffee or snacks for me," I say again. "I want to be hungry for supper."

"I don't think it'll be a typical spread tonight. Mom's been tired."

"You don't think she'll mind, though, right? That I'm coming?"

"No, she'll be happy. She's happy. My folks want to meet you."

"It's all barns around here. Seriously."

I've seen more of them on this drive than I've seen in years. Maybe in my life. They all look the same. Some cows, some horses. Sheep. Fields. And barns. Such a big sky.

"There're no lights on these highways."

"Not enough traffic to warrant lighting the way," he says. "I'm sure you've noticed."

"Must get really dark at night."

"It does."

IT FEELS LIKE I'VE KNOWN Jake longer than I have. What has it been . . . a month? Six weeks, maybe seven? I should know exactly. I'll say seven weeks. We have a real connection, a rare and intense attachment. I've never experienced anything like it.

I turn in my seat toward Jake, grabbing my left leg and bringing it up under me like a cushion. "So how much have you told them about me?"

"My parents? Enough," he says. He gives me a quick look. I like the look. I smile. I'm very attracted to him.

"What did you tell them?"

"That I met a pretty girl who drinks too much gin."

"My parents don't know who you are," I say.

He thinks I'm joking. But I'm not. They have no idea he exists. I haven't told them about Jake, not even that I've met someone. Nothing. I kept thinking I might say something. I've had multiple opportunities. I just never felt certain enough to say anything.

Jake looks like he's going to speak but changes his mind. He

reaches out and turns up the radio. Just a bit. The only music we could find after scanning through several times was a country station. The old stuff. He nods with the track, humming along softly.

"I've never heard you hum before," I say. "That's a quality hum you have."

I don't think my parents will *ever* know about Jake, not now, not even retroactively. As we drive down a deserted country highway to his parents' farm, this thought makes me sad. I feel selfish, self-centered. I should tell Jake what I'm thinking. It's just very hard to talk about. Once I bring up these doubts, I can't go back.

I've more or less decided. I'm pretty sure I'm going to end it. That takes the pressure off meeting his parents. I'm curious to see what they're like, but now I also feel guilty. I'm sure he thinks my visiting his family's farm is a sign of commitment, that the relationship is expanding.

He's sitting here, beside me. What's he thinking about? He doesn't have a clue. It's not going to be easy. I don't want to hurt him.

"How do you know this song? And haven't we heard it already? Twice?"

"It's a country classic and I grew up on a farm. I know it by default."

He doesn't confirm that we've heard the song twice already. What kind of radio station plays the same song over again within the hour? I don't listen to the radio much anymore; maybe that's

what they do now. Maybe that's normal. I wouldn't know. Or maybe these old country songs all sound the same to me.

WHY CAN'T I REMEMBER ANYTHING about the last road trip I took? I couldn't even say when it was. I'm looking out the window, but not really looking at anything. Just passing time the way one does in a car. Everything goes by so much faster in a car.

Which is too bad. Jake told me all about the landscape here. He loves it. He said he misses it whenever he's away. Especially the fields and sky, he said. I'm sure it is beautiful, peaceful. But it's hard to tell from the moving car. I'm trying to take in as much as I can.

We drive by a deserted property with only the foundation of a farmhouse. Jake says it burned down about a decade ago. There's a decrepit barn behind the house and a swing set in the front yard. But the swing set looks new. Not old and rusty, not weather-beaten.

"What's with the new swing set?" I ask.

"What?"

"On that burned farm. No one lives there anymore."

"Let me know if you get cold. Are you cold?"

"I'm fine," I say.

The glass of the window is cool. I'm resting my head against it. I can feel the vibrations of the engine through the glass, each bump in the road. A gentle brain massage. It's hypnotic.

I don't tell him I'm trying not to think about the Caller. I don't want to think about the Caller or his message at all. Not tonight. I also don't want to tell Jake that I'm avoiding catching my reflection in the window. It's a no-mirrors day for me. Just like the day Jake and I met. These are thoughts I keep to myself.

Trivia night at the campus pub. The night we met. The campus pub isn't somewhere I spend a lot of time. I'm not a student. Not anymore. I feel old there. I've never eaten at the pub. The beer on tap tastes dusty.

I wasn't expecting to meet anyone that night. I was sitting with my friend. We weren't really into the trivia, though. We were sharing a pitcher, chatting.

I think the reason my friend wanted us to meet at the campus pub was because she thought I might meet a boy there. She didn't say that, but that's what I believe she was thinking. Jake and his friends were at the table beside us.

Trivia is not something I'm interested in. It's not *not* fun. It's just not my thing. I'd prefer to go somewhere a little less intense, or stay home. Beer at home never tastes dusty.

Jake's trivia team was called Brezhnev's Eyebrows. "Who's Brezhnev?" I asked him. It was loud in there and we were almost yelling at each other over the music. We'd been talking for a couple of minutes.

"He was a Soviet engineer, worked in metallics. Era of Stagnation. Had a couple of monster caterpillars for eyebrows."

This is what I'm talking about. Jake's team name. It was meant

to be funny, but also obscure enough to demonstrate a knowledge of the Soviet Communist Party. I don't know why, but this is the stuff that drives me nuts.

Team names are always like this. Or if not, then they're blatant sexual innuendos. Another team was named My Couch Pulls Out and So Do I!

I told Jake I didn't really like trivia, not at a place like this. He said, "It can be very nitpicky. It's a strange blend of competitiveness veiled as apathy."

Jake isn't striking, not really. He's handsome mostly in his irregularity. He wasn't the first guy I noticed that night. But he was the most interesting. I'm rarely tempted by stainless beauty. He seemed a little less part of the group, as if he'd been dragged there, as if the team depended on his answers. I was immediately attracted to him.

Jake is long and sloping and unequal, with jagged cheekbones. A little bit gaunt. I liked those skeletal cheekbones when I first saw them. His dark, full lips make up for his underfed look. Fat and meaty and collagenic, especially the bottom one. His hair was short and unkempt and maybe longer on one side, or texturally different, like he had distinct hairstyles on each side of his head. His hair was neither dirty nor recently washed.

He was clean-shaven and wore thin-framed silver glasses, the right arm of which he would absentmindedly adjust. Sometimes he would push them back up with his index finger on the bridge. I noticed that he had this tick: when he was concentrating on some-

thing, he would smell the back of one hand, or at least hold it under his nose. It's something he often still does. He wore a plain gray T-shirt, I think, maybe blue, and jeans. The shirt looked like it had been washed hundreds of times. He blinked a lot. I could tell he was shy. We could have sat there all night, beside each other, and he wouldn't have said a word to me. He smiled at me once, but that was it. If I'd left it up to him, we never would have met.

I could tell he wasn't going to say anything, so I talked first.

"You guys are doing pretty well." That was the first thing I said to Jake.

He held up his beer glass. "We're helpfully fortified."

And that was it. Ice broken. We talked a bit more. Then, very casually, he said, "I'm a cruciverbalist."

I said something noncommittal, like "huh" or "yeah." I didn't know that word.

Jake said he wanted his team's name to be Ipseity. I didn't know what that word meant, either. And initially I thought about faking it. I could already tell, despite his caution and reticence, that he was exotically smart. He wasn't aggressive in any way. He wasn't trying to pick me up. No cheesy lines. He was just enjoying chatting. I got the feeling he didn't date all that much.

"I don't think I know that word," I said. "Or the other one." I decided that, like most men, he would probably like to tell me about it. He would like it better than if he thought I already knew the words and had an equally varied vocabulary.

"Ipseity is essentially just another way to say selfhood or individuality. It's from the Latin *ipse*, which means self."

I know this part sounds pedantic and lecture-y and off-putting, but trust me, it wasn't. Not at all. Not from Jake. He had a gentleness, an appealing, natural meekness.

"I thought it would be a good name for our team, considering there are many of us but we aren't like any other team. And because we play under a single team name, it creates an identity of oneness. Sorry, I don't know if this makes any sense, and it's definitely boring."

We both laughed, and it felt like we were alone together in there, in that pub. I drank some beer. Jake was funny. Or he at least had a sense of humor. I still didn't think he was as funny as me. Most men I meet aren't.

Later in the night, he said, "People just aren't very funny. Not really. Funny is rare." He said it as if he'd known exactly what I'd been thinking earlier.

"I don't know if that's true," I said. I liked hearing such a definitive statement about "people." There was deep confidence bubbling just under his veneer of restraint.

When I could tell he and his teammates were getting ready to leave, I thought about asking for his number or giving him mine. I desperately wanted to but just couldn't. I didn't want him to feel like he had to call. I wanted him to want to call, of course. I really did. But I settled on the likelihood that I would see him around. It was a university town, not a big city. I'd bump into him. As it turned out, I didn't have to wait for chance.

He must have slipped the note into my purse when he said good night. I found it when I got home:

If I had your number, we could talk, and I'd tell you something funny.

He'd written his number at the bottom of the note.

Before going to bed I looked up *cruciverbalist*. I laughed and believed him.

—I still don't understand. How could something like this happen?

—We're all in shock.

—Nothing so horrible has ever happened around here.

—No, not like this.

—In all the years I've worked here.

—I would think not.

—I didn't sleep last night. Not a wink.

—Me neither. Couldn't get comfortable. I can barely eat. You should have seen my wife when I told her. I thought she was going to be sick.

—How could he actually do it, go through with it? You don't do that on a whim. You couldn't.

—It's scary is what it is. Scary and disturbing.

—So did you know him? Were you close, or . . . ?

—No, no. Not close. I don't think anyone was close with him. He was a loner. That was his nature. Kept to himself. Standoffish. Some knew him better. But . . . you know.

—It's crazy. It doesn't seem real.

—It's one of those terrible things, but unfortunately it's very real.

"**H**ow are the roads?"

"Not bad," he says. "A little slick."

"Glad it's not snowing."

"Hopefully it won't start."

"It looks cold out there."

Individually, we're both unspectacular. It seems noteworthy. Combining our ingredients, Jake's lean height with my overt shortness, makes no sense. Alone in a crowd, I feel condensed, *overlook-able*. Jake, despite his height, also blends into a crowd. When we're together, though, I notice people looking at us. Not at him or at me: at us. Individually, I blend in. So does he. As a couple, we stand out.

Within six days of meeting at the pub, we'd had three proper meals together, gone for two walks, met for coffee, and watched a movie. We talked all the time. We'd been intimate. Jake has told me twice after seeing me naked that I remind him—in a good way, he stressed—of young Uma Thurman, a "compressed" Uma Thurman. He called me "compressed." That was the word. His word.

He's never called me sexy. Which is fine. He's called me pretty and he said "beautiful" once or twice, the way guys do. Once he

called me therapeutic. I'd never heard that from anyone before. It was right after we'd fooled around.

I thought it might happen—fooling around—but it wasn't planned. We'd just started making out on my couch after dinner. I'd made soup. For dessert we were splitting a bottle of gin. We were passing it back and forth, taking swigs right from the bottle like high school kids getting drunk before a dance. This instance felt much more urgent than the other times we'd made out. When the bottle was half-finished, we moved to the bed. He took off my top, and I unzipped his pants. He let me do what I wanted.

He kept saying, "Kiss me, kiss me." Even if I stopped for only three seconds. "Kiss me," again and again. Other than that, he was quiet. The lights were off, and I could barely hear him breathing.

I couldn't see him very well.

"Let's use our hands," he said. "Only our hands."

I thought we were about to have sex. I didn't know what to say. I went along with it. I'd never done that before. When we were finished he collapsed on top of me. We stayed like that for a bit, eyes closed, breathing. Then he rolled over and sighed.

I don't know how long it was after that, but eventually Jake got up and went to the bathroom. I lay there, watching him walk, listening to the tap running. I heard the toilet flush. He was in there for a while. I was looking at my toes, wiggling them.

I was thinking then that I should tell him about the Caller. But I just couldn't. I wanted to forget about it. Telling him would make it more serious than I wanted it to be. That was the closest I came to telling him.

I was lying there alone when a memory came to mind. When I was very young, maybe six or seven, I woke up one night and saw a man at my window. I hadn't thought about that in a long time. I don't often talk—or even think—about it. It's sort of a nebulous, patchy memory. But the parts I recall, I remember with clarity. This is not a story I offer up at dinner parties. I'm not sure what people would make of it. I'm not sure I know what to make of it myself. I don't know why it came to mind that night.

HOW DO WE KNOW WHEN something is menacing? What cues us that something is not innocent? Instinct always trumps reason. At night, when I wake up alone, the memory still terrifies me. It scares me more the older I get. Each time I remember it, it seems worse, more sinister. Maybe each time I remember it, I make it worse than it was. I don't know.

I woke up for no reason that night. It's not like I had to go to the bathroom. My room was very quiet. There was no coming to. I was immediately wide-awake. This was unusual for me. It always takes me a few seconds, or even minutes, to come to. This time, I woke up like I'd been kicked.

I was lying on my back, which was also unusual. I normally sleep on my side or stomach. The covers were up around me, tight, like I'd just been tucked in. I was hot, sweating. My pillow was moist. My door was closed, and the night-light that I usually left on was off. The room was dark.

The overhead fan was on high. It was spinning fast, I remember that part well. Really spinning. It seemed like it might fly off the ceiling. It was the only sound I could hear—the fan's metronomic motor and blades cutting through the air.

It wasn't a new house, and I could always hear something—pipes, or creaking, something—whenever I woke up in the night. It was strange that I couldn't hear anything else at that moment. I lay there listening, alert, addled.

And that's when I saw him.

My room was at the back of the house. It was the only bedroom on the ground floor. The window was in front of me. It wasn't wide or tall. The man was just standing there. Outside.

I couldn't see his face. It was beyond the window frame. I could see his torso, just half of it. He was swaying slightly. His hands were moving, rubbing each other from time to time, as if he was trying to warm them. I remember that vividly. He was very tall, very skinny. His belt—I remember his worn black belt—was fastened so that the excess part hung down like a tail in the front. He was taller than anyone I'd ever seen.

For a long time I watched him. I didn't move. He stayed where he was, too, right up against the window, his hands still moving over each other. He looked like he was taking a break from some kind of physical work.

But the longer I watched him, the more it seemed—or felt—like he could see me, even with his head and eyes above the top of the window. It didn't make sense. None of it did. If I couldn't see his eyes, how could he see me? I knew it wasn't a dream. It

wasn't *not* a dream, either. He was watching me. That's why he was there.

Soft music played, from outside, but I can't remember it clearly. I could barely hear it. And it wasn't noticeable when I first woke up. But I came to hear it after seeing the man. I'm not sure if it was recorded music or humming. A long time elapsed this way, I think, many minutes, maybe an hour.

And then the man waved. I wasn't expecting it. I honestly don't know if it was definitely a wave or a movement of his hand. Maybe it was just a wavelike gesture.

The wave changed everything. It had an effect of malice, as if he were suggesting I could never be completely on my own, that he would be around, that he would be back. I was suddenly afraid. The thing is, that feeling is just as real to me now as it was then. The visuals are just as real.

I closed my eyes. I wanted to call out but didn't. I fell asleep. When I finally opened my eyes, it was morning. And the man was gone.

After that, I thought it would reoccur. That he would appear again, watching. But it didn't. Not at my window, anyhow.

But I always felt like the man was there. The man is always there.

THERE HAVE BEEN TIMES I think I saw him. I'd pass a window, usually at night, and there'd be a tall man sitting with his legs crossed outside my house on the bench. He was still and looking my way. I'm not sure how a man sitting on a bench is pernicious, but he was.

He was far enough away that it was hard to see his face or know for sure if he was looking at me. I hated when I saw him. It didn't happen often. But I hated it. There was nothing I could do about it. He wasn't doing anything wrong. But he also wasn't doing anything at all. Not reading. Not talking. Just sitting there. Why was he there? That was probably the worst part. It may have all been in my head. These kinds of abstractions can seem most real.

I was lying on my back, as Jake had left me, when he returned from the bathroom. The covers were messed up. One of the pillows was on the floor. The way our clothes lay in messy heaps around the bed made the room look like a crime scene.

He stood at the foot of the bed without saying anything for what felt like an unnaturally long time. I'd seen him lying down naked but never standing. I pretended not to look. His body was pale, lean, and veiny. He found his underwear on the floor, pulled them on, and climbed back into bed.

"I want to stay here tonight," he said. "This is so nice. I don't want to leave you."

For some reason, right at that moment, as he slid up next to me, his foot rubbing up against mine, I wanted to make him jealous. I'd never felt such a strong urge before. It arrived out of nowhere.

I glanced at him beside me, lying on his stomach, his eyes closed. We both had sweaty hair. His face, like mine, was flushed.

"That was so nice," I said, tickling his lower back with the tips of my fingers. He moaned in agreement. "My last boyfriend . . .

there was no . . . a real connection is rare. Some relationships are all physical, only physical. It's an extreme physical release and nothing more. You might be all over each other, but that kind of thing doesn't last."

I still don't know why I said it. It wasn't entirely true, and why would I bring up another boyfriend in that moment? Jake didn't react. Not at all. He just lay there, turned on his side to face me, and said, "Keep doing that. It feels good. I like when you touch me. You're very tender. You're therapeutic."

"You feel good, too," I said.

Five minutes later, Jake's breathing changed. He'd fallen asleep. I was hot and kept the covers off me. The room was dark, but my eyes had adjusted; I could still see my toes. I heard my phone ring in the kitchen. It was really late. Too late for anyone to be calling. I didn't get up to answer it. I couldn't fall asleep. I tossed and turned. It rang three more times. We stayed in bed.

When I woke up in the morning, later than usual, Jake was gone. I was under the covers. I had a headache and a dry mouth. The bottle of gin was on the floor, empty. I was wearing underwear and a tank top but had no memory of ever putting them on.

I should have told Jake about the Caller. I realize that now. It's something I should have told him about when it started. I should have told *someone*. But I didn't. I didn't think it was anything significant until it was. Now I know better.

The first time he called, it was just a wrong number. That's all. Nothing serious. Nothing to be worried about. That call came the same night I met Jake at the pub. Wrong numbers don't happen

often, but they aren't unheard of. The call woke me from a deep sleep. The only strange part was the Caller's voice—a strained timbre and subdued, gradual delivery.

Right from the start, from that first week with Jake, even from the first date, I noticed odd little things about him. I don't like that I notice these things. But I do. Even now, in the car. I notice his smell. It's subtle. But in this enclosed space, it's there. It's not bad. I don't know how to describe it. It's just Jake's smell. So many small details that we learn in such short periods of time. It's been weeks, not years. There are obviously things I don't know about him. And there are things he doesn't know about me. Like the Caller.

The Caller was a man, I could hear that, middle-aged at least, probably older, but with a distinctly feminine voice, almost as if he was putting on a flat female intonation, or at least making his voice higher pitched, more delicate. It was unpleasantly distorted. It was a voice I didn't recognize. It wasn't someone I knew.

For a long time, I listened to that first message over and over, seeing if I could detect anything familiar. I couldn't. I still can't.

After that first call, when I explained to the Caller that it must be a wrong number, he said, "I'm sorry," in his scratchy, effeminate voice. He waited for another beat or two and then hung up. I forgot about it after that.

The next day I saw I had two missed calls. Both were received in the middle of the night when I was asleep. I checked my missed-calls list and saw it was the same number as the wrong number from the day before. That was weird. Why would he call back? But what was really weird, and inexplicable—and this still

makes me upset—was that the calls had come from my own number.

I didn't believe it at first. I almost didn't recognize my number. I did a double take. I thought it was an error. It had to be. But I double-checked and made sure I was looking at the missed-calls list and not something else. It was definitely the missed-calls list. There it was. My number.

It wasn't until three or four days later that the Caller left his first voice message. That's when it really started to get eerie. I still have that message saved. I have them all. He's left seven. I don't know why I've kept them. Maybe because I think I might tell Jake.

I reach down into my purse and take my phone out, dial.

"Who're you calling?" asks Jake.

"Just checking my messages."

I listen to the first saved message. It's the first voice message the Caller left.

There's only one question to resolve. I'm scared. I feel a little crazy. I'm not lucid. The assumptions are right. I can feel my fear growing. Now is the time for the answer. Just one question. One question to answer.

The messages aren't obviously aggressive or threatening. Neither is the voice. I don't think. Now I'm not so sure. They're definitely sad. The Caller sounds sad, maybe a bit frustrated. I don't know what his words mean. They seem nonsensical, but they also aren't babble. And they're always the same. Word for word.

.   .   .

SO THIS IS BASICALLY THE only other interesting thing in my life right now. That I've been seeing Jake and that someone else, another man, has been leaving me unusual voice messages. I don't often have secrets.

Sometimes when I'm in bed, sound asleep, I'll wake up and see that I have a missed call, often around 3:00 a.m. He usually calls in the middle of the night. And the call always comes from my number.

Once he called when Jake and I were watching a movie in bed. When my number came up, I didn't say anything but pretended I was chewing and handed the phone to Jake. He answered and said it was some old woman who'd called the wrong number. He seemed unconcerned. We kept watching the movie. I didn't sleep very well that night.

Since these calls have started, I've had nightmares, really scary dreams, and have woken up twice in the middle of the night in a bit of a panic, feeling like someone is in my apartment. That's never happened to me before. It's a terrible feeling. For a second or two, it feels like someone is right in the room, standing in the corner, very close, watching me. It's so real and frightening. I can't move.

I'm half-asleep, but after a minute or so, I fully wake up and go to the bathroom. It's always very quiet in my apartment. I run the water in the sink and it sounds extra loud because everything is so quiet. My heart's pounding. I'm very sweaty, and once had to change pajamas because they were so wet. I don't usually sweat, not like that. It's really not a nice feeling. It's too late to tell Jake any of this. I just feel a little more on edge than I usually am.

. . .

ONE NIGHT, WHILE I SLEPT, the Caller called twelve times. He didn't leave a message that night. But there were twelve missed calls. All from my number.

Most people would have done something about the issue after that, but I didn't. And what could I do? I couldn't call the police. He'd never threatened me or said anything violent or harmful. That's what I find so bizarre, that he doesn't want to talk. I guess I should say he *only* wants to talk. He never wants to converse. Anytime I've tried to answer one of his calls, he just hangs up. He prefers leaving his cryptic message.

Jake isn't paying attention. He's driving, so I listen to the message again.

There's only one question to resolve. I'm scared. I feel a little crazy. I'm not lucid. The assumptions are right. I can feel my fear growing. Now is the time for the answer. Just one question. One question to answer.

I've listened to it so many times. Over and over.

All of a sudden it had gone too far. It was the same message as it had always been, word for word, but this time there was something new at the end. The last message I got changed things. It was the worst. It was really creepy. I couldn't sleep at all that night. I felt scared and stupid for not putting a stop to the calls sooner. I felt stupid for not telling Jake. I'm still upset about it.

There's only one question to resolve. I'm scared. I feel a little crazy. I'm not lucid. The assumptions are right. I can feel my fear

growing. Now is the time for the answer. Just one question. One question to answer.

And then . . .

Now I'm going to say something that will upset you: I know what you look like. I know your feet and hands and your skin. I know your head and your hair and your heart. You shouldn't bite your nails.

I decided I definitely had to answer the next time he called. I had to tell him to stop. Even if he didn't say anything back, I could tell him that. Maybe that would be enough.

The phone rang.

"Why are you calling me? How did you get my number? You can't keep doing this," I said. I was mad and scared. This didn't feel like a random thing anymore. It didn't feel like he'd just dialed a number off the top of his head. It wasn't going to stop. He wasn't going to go away, and he wanted something. What did he want from me? Why me?

"This is about you. I can't help you!"

I was yelling.

"But you called me," he said.

"What?"

I hung up and threw my phone down. My chest was heaving.

I know it was just a stupid fluke, but I've been biting my nails since fifth grade.

—The night you called, we were having a dinner party. I'd made a pecan galette with salted caramel sauce for dessert. That call. The whole night was ruined for everyone after we heard. I can still remember every word of your call.

—The kids were out when I heard. I called you right away.

—Was he depressed or sick? Do we know if he was depressed?

—Apparently he wasn't on any antidepressants. He was keeping secrets, though. I'm sure there were more.

—Yeah.

—If we'd only known how serious it was. If only there'd been some signs. There are always signs. People don't just do that.

—This wasn't a rational person.

—That's true, that's a good point.

—He's not like us.

—No, no. Not like us at all.

—If you have nothing, there's nothing to lose.

—Yeah. Nothing to lose.

I think a lot of what we learn about others isn't what they tell us. It's what we observe. People can tell us anything they want. As Jake pointed out once, every time someone says "Pleased to meet you," they're actually thinking something different, making some judgment. Feeling "pleased" is never exactly what they're thinking or feeling, but that's what they say, and we listen.

Jake told me our relationship has its own valence. *Valence.* That's the word he used.

If that's true, then relationships can change from one afternoon to evening, from hour to hour. Lying in bed is one thing. When we eat breakfast together and when it's early, we don't speak a lot. I like to talk, even just a bit. It helps me wake up. Especially if the conversation is funny. Nothing wakes me up like a laugh, really, even just one big laugh, as long as it's sincere. It's better than caffeine.

Jake prefers to eat his cereal or toast and read, mostly in quiet. He's always reading. Lately it's that Cocteau book. He must have reread it five times by now.

But he also just reads whatever's available. At first I thought he was quiet at breakfast because he was so into whatever book he

was reading. I could understand that, though it's not how I operate. I wouldn't ever read this way. I like to know I have a good bit of time set aside for reading, to really get into the story. I don't like reading and eating, not together.

But it's the reading just for the sake of it that I find irritating. Jake will read anything—a newspaper, a magazine, a cereal box, a crappy flyer, a take-out menu, anything.

"Hey, do you think secrets are inherently unfair, or bad or immoral in a relationship?" I ask.

He's caught off guard. He looks at me, then back to the road.

"I don't know. It would depend on the secret. Is it significant? Is there more than one secret? How many are there? And what is being hidden? All relationships have secrets, though, don't you think? Even in lifelong relationships, and fifty-year marriages, there are secrets."

On the fifth morning we had breakfast together I stopped trying to start up a discussion. I didn't make any jokes. I sat. I ate cereal. Jake's brand. I looked around the room. I watched him. I observed. I thought: This is good. This is how we *really* get to know each other.

He was reading a magazine. There was a faint white film or residue under his bottom lip, concentrated in the corners of his mouth, in the valley where the top and bottom lips meet. This happened most mornings, this white lip film. After he showered, it was usually gone.

Was it toothpaste? Was it from breathing out of his mouth all night? Was it the mouth equivalent of eye boogers? When he read,

he chewed very slowly, as if to conserve energy, as if concentrating on the words slowed his ability to swallow. Sometimes there was a long delay between the last revolution of his jaw and his swallow.

He'd wait for a bit and then dig out another overflowing spoonful from his bowl, holding it up absentmindedly. I thought he might drip milk onto his chin; each spoon was so full. But he didn't. He got it all into his mouth without a single drip. He rested the spoon in the bowl and wiped at his chin, even though there was nothing on it. It was all done distractedly.

His jaw is very taut and muscular. Even now. Even while sitting, driving.

How can I stop myself from thinking about eating breakfast with him twenty or thirty years from now? Would he still get that white residue every day? Would it be worse? Does everyone in a relationship think about this stuff? I watched him swallow—that prominent Adam's apple, more a gnarled peach pit stuck in his throat.

Sometimes post-eating, usually after a large meal, his body makes sounds like a cooling car after a long drive. I can hear liquids shifting through small spaces. This doesn't happen so much at breakfast, more often after supper.

I hate to dwell on these things. They're unimportant and banal, but now's the time to think about them before this relationship gets any more serious. This makes me crazy, though, right? I'm crazy for thinking about this stuff?

Jake is smart. He'll be a full professor before long. Full tenure and all that. This stuff's appealing. It makes a good life. He's tall.

He has his clumsy physical appeal. He's attractively misanthropic. All things I would have wanted in a husband when I was younger. Checks in all the boxes. I'm just not sure what any of this means now that I'm watching him eat cereal and hearing his body make hydraulic noises.

"Do you think your parents have secrets?" I ask.

"Absolutely. I'm sure they do. They'd have to."

The weirdest part—and it's some pretty unalloyed irony, as Jake would say—is that I can't say anything to him about my doubts. They have everything to do with him, and he's the one person I'm not comfortable talking to about them. I won't say anything until I'm sure it's over. I can't. What I'm questioning involves both of us, affects both of us, yet I can only decide alone. What does that say about relationships? Another in the long line of early-relationship contradictions.

"Why all the questions about secrets?"

"No reason," I say. "Just thinking."

Maybe I should simply enjoy this trip. Not overthink it. Get out of my own head. Have fun; let things happen naturally.

I don't know what this means—"let things happen naturally"—but I've heard it over and over. People say it to me a lot about relationships. Isn't that what we're doing? I'm letting myself consider these thoughts. It's natural. I'm not going to prevent doubts from blooming. Wouldn't that be *more* unnatural?

I ask myself what my reasons are for ending things and have trouble coming up with anything substantial. But how can you not ask this question in a relationship? What's here to keep it going? To make it worthwhile? Mostly, I just think I'd be better off without Jake, that it makes more sense than going on. I'm not certain, though. How can I be certain? I've never broken up with a boyfriend before.

Most relationships I've been in were like a carton of milk reaching its expiration date. It gets to a certain point and just sours, not inducing sickness but enough to notice a change in flavor. Maybe instead of wondering about Jake, I should be questioning my ability to experience passion. This could all be my fault.

"Even when it's cold like this, if it's clear," Jake's saying, "I don't mind. You can always bundle up. There's something about the deep cold that's refreshing."

"Summer's better," I say. "I hate being cold. We still have at least another month before spring. It's going to be a long month."

"I saw Venus without a telescope one summer."

Such a Jake thing to say.

"It was one night around sunset. It wasn't going to be visible from Earth again for more than a hundred years. It was this very rare planetary alignment that coordinated the sun and Venus, so you could see it as a tiny black dot when it passed between Earth and the sun. It was really cool."

"If I'd known you then, you could have told me about it. I missed out."

"That's the thing; no one seemed to care," he says. "It was so strange. A chance to see Venus, and most people were watching TV. No offense if that's what you were doing."

I know Venus is the second planet from the sun. I don't know much about it beyond that. "Do you like Venus?" I ask.

"Sure."

"Why? Why do you like it?"

"One day on Venus is like one hundred fifteen Earth days. Its atmosphere is made up of nitrogen and carbon dioxide and it has an iron core. It's also full of volcanoes and solidified lava, sort of like Iceland. I should know its orbital velocity, but I'd be making it up."

"That's pretty good," I say.

"But what I like most is that apart from the sun and moon, it's the brightest object in the sky. Most people don't know that."

I like when he talks like this.

I want to hear more. "Were you always interested in space?"

"I don't know," he says. "I guess so. In space, everything has its relative position. Space is an entity, right, but also limitless. It's less dense the farther out you go, but you can always keep going. There's no definitive border between the start and the end. We'll never fully understand or know it. We can't."

"You don't think?"

"Dark matter makes up the majority of all matter, and it's still a mystery."

"Dark matter?"

"It's invisible. It's all the extra mass we can't see that makes the formation of galaxies and the rotational velocities of stars around galaxies mathematically possible."

"I'm glad we don't know everything."

"You're glad?"

"That we don't know all the answers, that we can't explain it all, like space. Maybe we're not supposed to know all the answers. Questions are good. They're better than answers. If you want to know more about life, how we work, how we progress, it's questions that are important. That's what pushes and stretches our intellect. I think questions make us feel less lonely and more connected. It's not always about knowing. I appreciate not knowing. Not knowing is human. That's how it should be, like space. It's unsolvable, and it's dark," I say, "but not entirely."

He laughs at this, and I feel silly for saying what I said.

"I'm sorry," he says. "I'm not laughing at you, it's just funny. I haven't heard anyone say it like that before."

"But it's true, isn't it?"

"Yeah. It's dark, but not entirely. It's true. And that's kind of a nice idea."

—Some of the rooms were vandalized, I heard.

—Yup, paint on the floor, red paint; some water damage. Did you know he put a chain on the door?

—Why did he do it in here?

—To make some selfish, twisted point, maybe. I don't know.

—He wasn't a vandal type, was he?

—No, but the strange thing is he'd started writing graffiti on some of the walls. We all knew it was him. People saw him doing it. He denied it, but volunteered to clean it off every time.

—That's weird.

—That's not even the weird part.

—What?

—The strange part was that he wrote the same thing every time. The graffiti. Just one sentence.

—What was it?

—"There's only one question we need to resolve."

—There's only one question we need to resolve?

—Yup. That's what he wrote.

—What's the one question?

—I have no idea.

"**W**e still have a while to go, right?"

"Yeah, a bit longer."

"How about a story?"

"A story?"

"Yeah, to pass the time," I say. "I'll tell you a story. A true one. One you've never heard. It's your kind of story. I think you'll like it."

I turn the music down a little.

"Sure," he says.

"It's about when I was younger, a teenager."

I look over at him. At a table, he often looks slouchy and uncomfortable. Driving, he looks too long to fit comfortably behind the wheel, but his posture is good. I'm attracted to Jake's physical stature through his intellect. His sharpness of mind makes his lankiness appealing. They're connected. At least to me.

"Ready," he says. "For story time."

I clear my throat super dramatically.

"Okay. I'd been sheltering my head with some newspaper. Seriously. What? Why are you smiling? It was pouring. I'd grabbed the paper from an empty seat on the bus. My instructions had been

simple: arrive at the house at ten thirty and you will be greeted in the driveway. I was told I didn't need to ring the bell. You're listening, right?"

He nods, still looking out the windshield at the road ahead.

"When I got there, I had to wait for a while—minutes, not seconds. When the door finally opened, a man I'd never met poked his head out. He looked up at the sky and then said something like he hoped I hadn't been waiting long. He held out a hand palm up. He looked exhausted, as if he'd been awake for days. Big dark bags under both eyes. Stubble on his cheeks and chin. Bedhead. I tried to glance past him. The door was open slightly, a crack.

"He said: 'I'm Doug. Gimme a minute, take the keys,' and he flipped me the keys, which I caught like a punch, both my hands against my stomach. The door slammed shut.

"I didn't move, not at first. I was stunned. Who was this guy? I really didn't know anything about him. We'd talked on the phone, that's it. I looked down at the metal key chain in my hands, which was just a large letter *J*."

I stop. I glance at Jake. "You look bored," I say. "I know I'm including lots of details, but I remember them, and I'm trying to tell a proper story. Is it weird that I remember these details? Is it boring because I'm telling you everything?"

"Just tell your story. Pretty much all memory is fiction and heavily edited. So just keep going."

"I'm not sure I agree with that, about memory. But I know what you mean," I say.

"Keep going," he says. "I'm listening."

"It was another eight minutes, at least two watch checks, before Doug reappeared. He fell into the passenger seat with a big exhale. He'd changed into worn blue jeans with holes in the knees and a plaid shirt. The seats in his car were mottled with orange cat hair. There was cat hair everywhere."

"Mottled."

"Yes, mottled to the nth degree. He was also wearing a black baseball cap, tipped back on his head, with the word *Nucleus* embroidered on the front in white cursive lettering. He seemed better suited to sitting than standing or walking.

"He didn't say anything, so I started into the routine I'd been practicing with Dad. Slid the seat forward, adjusted the rearview mirror three times, and ensured the parking brake was released. I placed my hands at ten and two on the steering wheel and straightened my posture.

" 'I never like the rain,' Doug said. It was the first thing he said in the car. Nothing about instruction or how long I'd been practicing. I could tell how shy and almost nervous he was now that we were in the car together. His knee bobbed up and down. 'Is there somewhere you want me to start?' I asked. 'It's this rain,' he said, 'sort of throws things off. I think we'll have to wait it out.' Through the use of hand signals alone, Doug directed me to pull into the first lot on our left. It was a coffee shop parking lot. He asked if I wanted anything, a coffee or tea, and I told him I was fine. For a while we just sat there without talking, listening to the rain on the car. The engine was still on to keep the windows from fogging up, and I had the wipers set to a low speed. 'So how old are you?' he

asked. He thought maybe seventeen or eighteen. I told him sixteen.

" 'That's pretty old,' was what he said. His nails were like mini surfboards; long, narrow, dirty mini surfboards. His hands were those of an artist, a writer, not a driving instructor."

"If you need to take a break from the story to swallow or blink or breathe, go ahead," says Jake. "You're like Meryl Streep, fully committed to your role."

"I'll breathe when I'm done," I say. "He mentioned again that sixteen wasn't young, and that age was a strange, inaccurate umpire for maturity. Then he opened the glove box and took out a small book. 'I want to read you something,' he said, 'if you don't mind, since we're waiting and all.' He asked if I knew anything about Jung. I said, 'Not really,' which wasn't entirely true."

"Your driving instructor was a Jungian?"

"Just hold on. It took him a moment to find the place in the book. He cleared his throat and then read this line to me: 'The meaning of my existence is that life has addressed a question to me. Or, conversely, I myself am a question which is addressed to the world, and I must communicate my answer, for otherwise I am dependent upon the world's answer.' "

"Do you have that memorized?"

"Yeah."

"How?"

"He gave me the book. I kept it. I still have it somewhere. He was in a giving mood that day. He said experience wasn't just good for driving but for everything. 'Experience trumps age,' he said.

'We have to find ways to experience because that's how we learn, that's how we know.'"

"Such a weird lesson."

"I asked why he liked to teach driving. He said it wasn't his first choice for a job but that he had to do it for practical reasons. He said he'd grown to appreciate sitting in a car and talking to others. He said he liked puzzles. He said he liked driving and navigating with another person as a metaphor. He reminded me of the Cheshire Cat from *Alice in Wonderland*, except he was a shy version of the cat."

"It's funny," says Jake.

"What?"

"I was into Jung for a bit there, too. To really know ourselves we have to question ourselves. I always liked that idea. Anyway, sorry. Go on."

"Right. As we were waiting, he reached into his pocket and fished out two strange-looking candies. 'You keep that one,' he said, pointing to one of them. 'Save it for another rainy day.' He took the other candy and twisted open the shiny paper. He snapped it between his fingers, breaking it in two. He handed me the larger piece."

"Did you eat it?" asks Jake. "Wasn't it weird that this guy was offering you candy? And didn't it gross you out that he touched it?"

"I'm getting to all that. But yes, it was weird. And yes, I was grossed out. But I ate it."

"Continue."

"It didn't taste like anything. I moved the candy back and forth over my tongue, trying to decide if it was sweet at all. I couldn't tell if it was good or bad. He told me he got the candies from one of his students. He told me she'd been traveling somewhere in Asia, and that they were one of the most popular candies there. He said his student loved them but he didn't think they were anything special. He was chewing his candy, crunching it.

"Suddenly, I started to taste it. An unexpected tang, a tartness. It wasn't bad. I started to like it. He told me, 'You still don't know the most interesting part.' He said, 'All the wrappers on these candies print a few lines in English on the label. They've been directly translated, so they don't make much sense.' He took the wrapper back out of his pocket and unfolded it for me.

"I read aloud the words that were printed on the inside. I remember them word for word: '*You are the new man. How delicious cannot forget, special taste. Return the turn flavor.*'

"I reread those lines a few times, to myself, then once more aloud. He told me he unwrapped candies every now and then, not to eat, but just because he liked reading the verses, to think about them, trying to understand them. He said he wasn't a poetry man but these lines were as good as any poem he'd ever read. He said, 'There are certain things in life, not very many, that are real, confirmed cures for rainy days, for loneliness. Puzzles are like that. We each have to solve our own.' I'll never forget him saying that."

"It's memorable. I wouldn't forget it, either."

"By this point, we'd been in the parking lot for more than twenty minutes, and we still hadn't done any real driving. He told

me that the student who'd given him the candies was unique, that she was hopeless behind the wheel, a terrible driver. He said it didn't matter what tips he gave or that he repeated all the pointers over and over, she just couldn't get it. He said he knew from the first lesson that she was never going to pass her driver's test, that she was the worst driver in the world. Giving her lessons was pointless and borderline dangerous.

"He went on to say that regardless, he really looked forward to those lessons, and that he would have long, long chats with this girl, full-on discussions. He'd tell her about some of the things he'd been reading, and she'd tell him the same. It was a back-and-forth. He said she would sometimes say things that blew him away."

"Like what?" asks Jake. I can tell that although he's concentrating on driving, he is listening and alert. He's into the story, more than I thought he'd be.

My phone rings. I grab it from my purse, which is on the floor near my feet.

"Who's that?" asks Jake.

I see my own number displayed.

"Oh, it's just a friend. I don't need to answer."

"Good. Keep going with the story."

Why is he calling again? What does he want? "Right," I say, putting my phone back in my bag and turning back to the story.

"Okay, so. One day, out of the blue, this student told her driving instructor she was 'the best kisser in the world.' She just told him, like she thought he should know. She was so sure of it, and he said she was very convincing."

Jake readjusts his hands on the wheel, sits up even straighter. I hear my phone beep, indicating a message has been left.

"He told me he knew it seemed weird to talk about this. He may even have apologized, admitting he'd never told anyone else this detail. She swore this talent made her more powerful than money or intelligence or anything else. The fact that she was the best kisser in the world made her the center of the universe, in her words.

"He was looking for me to reply, or to say something. I didn't know what to say. So I told him what came to mind, that kissing involves two people. You can't be a singular person and be the best kisser. It's an action that requires two. 'So really,' I said, 'you would only be the best if the other person was also the best, which is impossible.' I told him, 'It's not like playing the guitar or something, where you're alone and you know you're good at it. It's not a solitary act. There need to be two best.'

"My answer seemed to bother him. He was visibly upset. He didn't like the idea that alone, you couldn't be the best kisser, that one was reliant on another kisser. And then he said, 'This is too much to overcome.' He said that would mean we'd always need someone else. But what if there wasn't someone else? What if we are all just alone?

"I didn't know what to say. Then he kind of snapped, as if we'd been in an argument. He said, 'It's stupid to try to wait the rain out.' He told me to take a right out of the parking lot. It was so strange. He indicated where I should go with various tilts of his head. He was quiet after that."

"Interesting," says Jake.

"I'm almost done."

"Go on."

"For the remainder of the lesson, Doug was twitchy in his seat and seemed disinterested in anything driving related. He offered some basic advice on driving technique, but mostly he looked out the windshield. This was my first and last driving lesson.

"Since it was still raining, he told me he'd drop me off at my place so I didn't have to wait for the bus. Very little was said. When we reached my house, I pulled up in front and told him I'd keep practicing with my dad. He said that was a good idea. I left him there and ran into the house.

"About a minute later—it wasn't long—I came back outside. He was still there in the car. He'd moved himself into the driver's seat and had the wheel in both hands. The seat was still positioned for me, as was the mirror. He was squished in tight. I signaled for him to lower the window. He slid the seat back first before rolling the window down. It was still normal then not to have power windows.

"Before it had fully reached the bottom, I slid my head into the car and gently placed a hand on his left shoulder. My hair was soaked. I had to make a point. I told him to shut his eyes for a second. My face was close to his. He did. He shut his eyes and sort of leaned toward me. And then . . ."

"What? I can't believe you did this," says Jake. "What the hell came over you?"

It's the most animated I've ever seen Jake. He's shocked, almost angry.

"I'm not sure. It just felt like I had to."

"This seems so unlike you. Did you ever see him after that?"

"No, I didn't. That was it."

"Huh," says Jake. "Is a second person required for there to be a best kisser? It's interesting. That's the kind of thing that can stay with you, that you can think about and obsess over."

Jake passes the slow-moving pickup in front of us. It's black, old. We've been following that truck for a while, pretty much for the entire story. I try to see the driver as we go by but can't make him out. There haven't been many cars with us on the road.

"What did you mean when you said all memory is fiction?" I ask.

"A memory is its own thing each time it's recalled. It's not absolute. Stories based on actual events often share more with fiction than fact. Both fictions and memories are recalled and retold. They're both forms of stories. Stories are the way we learn. Stories are how we understand each other. But reality happens only once."

This is when I'm most attracted to Jake. Right now. When he says things like "Reality happens only once."

"It's just weird, when you start thinking about it. We go see a movie and understand it's not real. We know it's people acting, reciting lines. It still affects us."

"So you're saying that it doesn't matter if the story I just told you is made up or if it actually happened?"

"Every story is made up. Even the real ones."

Another classic Jake line.

"I'll have to think about that."

"You know that song 'Unforgettable'?"

"Yeah," I say.

"How much is truly unforgettable?"

"I don't know. I'm not sure. I like the song, though."

"Nothing. Nothing is unforgettable."

"What?"

"That's the thing. Part of everything will always be forgettable. No matter how good or remarkable it is. It literally has to be. To be."

"That is the question?"

"Don't," says Jake.

I'm not sure what to say right then. I'm not sure how to respond.

For a while he doesn't say anything else. He just plays with his hair, curling a piece at the back of his head around his index finger the way he does, the way I like. And then, after a while, he looks at me.

"What would you say if I told you I'm the smartest human on earth?"

"Pardon?"

"I'm serious. And this is relevant to your story. Just answer."

I'd guess we've been driving for at least fifty minutes, probably longer. It's getting darker outside. There are no lights on in the car, beyond the dash and radio.

"What would I say?"

"Yeah. Would you laugh? Would you call me a liar? Would you get mad? Or would you just question the rationality of such a bold statement?"

"I guess I would say 'Pardon?'"

Jake laughs at this. Not a big laugh, but a small, sincere, ingested, Jake kind of laugh.

"Seriously. I'm saying it. You've heard me clearly. How do you respond?"

"Well, what you're saying is that you're the smartest man on earth?"

"Incorrect. The smartest *human*. And I'm not saying I *am*; I'm wondering how you would respond if I *did* say that. Take your time."

"Jake, come on."

"I'm being serious."

"I guess I'd say you're full of shit."

"Really?"

"Yeah. The smartest human on earth? It's ridiculous for so many reasons."

"What are the reasons?"

I lift my head, which had been resting on my hands, and look around, as if there's an audience present. Blurs of trees pass the window.

"Okay, let me ask you a question. Do you think you're the smartest human alive?"

"That's not an answer. That's a question."

"And I'm allowed to answer in the form of a question."

I know I'm opening myself to the obvious *Jeopardy!* joke as I say it, but Jake doesn't make it. Of course he doesn't.

"Why is it impossible that I'm the smartest human on earth beyond just saying that it's crazy?"

"I don't even know where to start."

"That's the whole point. You just assume it to be too far-fetched to be real. You can't perceive that someone you know, some regular dude sitting beside you in a car, is the smartest person. But why not?"

"Because what do you even mean by smart? Are you more book-smart than me? Maybe. But what about building a fence? Or knowing when to ask someone how they're doing or feeling compassion or knowing how to live with others, to connect with other people? Empathy is a big part of smarts."

"Of course it is," he says. "That's all part of my question."

"Fine. But still, I don't know, I mean, how could there even be a smartest person?"

"There has to be. Whatever algorithm you create, or whatever you decide makes up intelligence, someone has to meet those criteria more than everyone else. Someone has to be the smartest in the world. And what a burden it is. It really is."

"What does it matter? One smartest person?"

He leans a little toward me. "The most attractive thing in the world is the combination of confidence and self-consciousness. Blended together in the proper amounts. Too much of either and all is lost. And you were right, you know."

"Right? About what?"

"About the best kisser," he says. "Thankfully you can't be the best kisser alone. It's not like being the smartest."

He leans back his way, reasserts both hands on the wheel. I look out my window.

"And anytime you want to have a fence-building contest, just let me know," he says.

He never let me finish my story. I never kissed Doug after our lesson. Jake assumed. He assumed I kissed Doug. But a kiss needs two people who want to kiss, or it's something else.

Here's what really happened. I went back to the car that time. I leaned in the window and opened my hand, revealing the tiny wrinkled candy wrapper, the one Doug gave me. I uncrumpled it and read it:

My heart, my heart alone with its lapping waves of song, longs to touch this green world of the sunny day. Hello!

I still have the candy wrapper somewhere. I saved it. I don't know why. After reading those lines to Doug, I turned and ran back into my house. I never saw him again.

—He had keys. He wasn't scheduled to be here, but he had keys. He could do whatever he wanted.

—Wasn't there supposed to be some revarnishing done during the break?

—Yes, but that happened right at the start of the holidays. So the varnish would have time to dry. The varnish scent can be pretty strong.

—Toxic?

—Again, I'm not sure. Maybe, if that's all you were breathing.

—Are we going to see any autopsy results?

—I can look into that.

—Was it . . . messy?

—You can imagine.

—I can.

—We shouldn't get into the details right now.

—I hear they found a breathing apparatus, a gas mask, near the body?

—Yes, but it was an old one. It's unclear if it still worked.

—There's so much we don't know about what really happened in there.

—And the only one who could tell us is gone.

J ake has started talking about aging. I didn't see it coming. It's not a topic we've ever discussed before. "It's just one of those culturally misunderstood things."

"But you think getting old is good?"

"I do. It is. First of all, it's inevitable. It just seems negative because of our overwhelming obsession with youth."

"Yeah, I know. They're all positives. But what about your boyish good looks? You can kiss those good-bye. Are you prepared to be fat and bald?"

"Whatever we lose physically as we age is worth it, given what we gain. It's a fair trade-off."

"Yeah, yeah, I'm with you," I say. "I actually want to be older. I'm happy to age, seriously."

"I keep hoping for some gray hairs. Some wrinkles. I'd like to have some laugh lines. I guess, more than anything, I want to be myself," he says. "I want to be. To be me."

"How so?"

"I want to understand myself and recognize how others see me. I want to be comfortable being myself. How I reach that is

almost less important, right? It means something to get to the next year. It's significant."

"I think that's why so many people rush into marriage and stay in shitty relationships, regardless of age, because they aren't comfortable being alone."

I can't say this to Jake and I don't, but maybe it's better to be alone. Why abandon the routine we each master? Why give up the opportunity for many diverse relationships in exchange for one? There's plenty of good with coupling up, I get it, but is it *better*? When single, I tend to focus on how much the company of someone would improve my life, increase my happiness. But does it?

"Do you care if I turn this down a bit?" I ask, adjusting the radio before waiting for his reply. I've turned it down multiple times on this drive; Jake keeps turning it back up. I think he might be a bit deaf. At least some of the time. It's like all absentminded ticks—there sometimes, but other times, not so much.

One night, I had a headache. We were chatting on the phone and he was planning on coming over to hang out. I asked him to bring me a couple of Advil. I wasn't sure he'd remember, even though I'd repeated it. It was one of the bad headaches I've been getting recently. I assumed he'd forget. Jake forgets things. He can be bit of a scatterbrained professor cliché.

When he arrived at my place, I didn't say anything about the pills. I didn't want him to feel bad if he'd forgotten. He didn't say anything, either. Not at first. We were talking about something else, I can't remember, and he just said out of the blue, "Your pills."

He pushed a hand into his pocket. He had to straighten out his legs to get his hand in. I watched him.

"Here," he'd said.

He didn't just pull out two pills from his linty pocket. He handed me a small ball of Kleenex, all wrapped up in itself and sealed with a single piece of tape. The package looked like a large white Hershey's Kiss. I undid the tape. Inside were my pills. Three of them. An extra, in case I needed it.

"Thanks," I said. I went into the bathroom for water. I didn't say anything to Jake, but to me, the wrapping was significant. Protecting the pills like that. He wouldn't have done that for himself.

It threw me off a bit, made me rethink things. I was going to break up with him that night—maybe. It's possible I was. I wasn't planning to. But it could have happened. But he put my pills in the Kleenex.

Are small, critical actions enough? Small gestures make us feel good—about ourselves, about others. Small things connect us. They feel like everything. A lot depends on them. It's not unlike religion and God. We believe in certain constructs that help us understand life. Not only to understand it, but as a means of providing comfort. The idea that we are better off with one person for the rest of our lives is not an innate truth of existence. It's a belief we want to be true.

Forfeiting solitude, independence, is a much greater sacrifice than most of us realize. Sharing a habitat, a life, is for sure harder than being alone. In fact, coupled living seems virtually impossible, doesn't it? To find another person to spend all your life with?

To age with and change with? To see every day, to respond to their moods and needs?

It's funny that Jake brought up intelligence earlier. His question about the smartest human in the world. It's like Jake knew I've been thinking about that. I've been thinking about all of these things. Is intelligence always good? I wonder. What if intelligence is wasted? What if intelligence leads to more loneliness rather than to fulfillment? What if instead of productivity and clarity it generates pain, isolation, and regret? It's been on my mind a lot, Jake's intelligence. Not just now. I've been thinking about it for a while.

His intelligence initially attracted me, but in a committed relationship, is it a good thing for me? Would someone less intelligent be harder to live with or easier? I'm talking long-term here, not just a few months or years. Logic and intelligence aren't linked with generosity and empathy. Or are they? Not his intelligence, anyway. He's a literal, linear, intellectual thinker. How does this make thirty or forty or fifty years together more appealing?

I turn to him. "I know you don't like talking about actual work stuff, but I've never seen your lab. What's it like?"

"What do you mean?"

"It's hard for me to envision where you work."

"Picture a lab. That's pretty much it."

"Does it smell like chemicals? Are there lots of people around?"

"I don't know. I guess so, yeah, usually."

"But you don't have any problems being distracted, or concentrating?"

"Usually it's fine. Every now and then there's a disturbance or something, someone talking on the phone or laughing. Once I had to 'shhh' a colleague. That's never fun."

"I know how you are when you get focused."

"At those times I don't even want to hear the clock."

I think this car must be dusty, or maybe it's just the vents. But my eyes feel dry in here. I adjust the vent, aiming it fully toward the floor.

"Give me a virtual tour."

"Of the lab?"

"Yeah."

"Now?"

"You can do that and drive. What would you show me if I visited you at work?"

For a while he doesn't say anything. He just looks straight ahead, through the windshield.

"First, I'd show you the protein crystallography room." He doesn't look at me as he talks.

"Okay," I say. "Good."

I know his work involves ice crystals and proteins. That's about it. I know he's working on a postdoc and thesis.

"I'd show you the two crystallization robots that allow us to screen a large area of crystallization space, using sub-microliter volumes of difficult-to-express recombinant proteins."

"See," I say, "I like hearing this."

I really do.

"You'd probably be interested in the microscope room that contains the setup of our three-color TIRF, or total internal reflection fluorescence, as well as the spinning disk microscope that allows us to accurately track fluorescently tagged single molecules, either in vitro or in vivo with nanometer precision."

"Go on."

"I'd show you our temperature-controlled incubators in which we grow large volumes, more than twenty liters, of yeast and *E. coli* cultures that have been genetically engineered to overexpress a protein of our choosing."

As he talks, I'm studying his face, his neck, his hands. I can't help myself.

"I'd show you our two systems—AKTA FPLC, fast protein liquid chromatography—that allow us to purify any protein quickly and accurately using any combination of affinity, ion exchange, and gel permeation chromatographies."

I want to kiss him as he drives.

"I'd show you the tissue culture room where we grow and maintain various mammalian cell lines either for transfection of specific genes or harvesting of cell lysate . . ."

He pauses.

"Go on," I say. "And then?"

"And then I feel like you'd be bored and ready to leave."

I could say something to him right now. We're alone in the car. It's the perfect time. I could say I've been thinking about a relationship in the context of only myself and what everything means

to me. Or I could ask if this is irrelevant because a relationship can't be understood sliced in two. Or I could be completely honest and say, "I'm thinking of ending things." But I don't. I don't say any of that.

Maybe going to meet his parents, seeing where he comes from, where he grew up, maybe that will help me decide what to do.

"Thank you," I say. "For the tour."

I watch him drive. For now. That messy, slightly curled hair. That fucking exquisite posture. I think about those three tiny pills. It changes everything. It was so nice of him to wrap them up for me.

WE'D KNOWN EACH OTHER FOR only about two weeks when Jake left town for two nights. We'd seen each other or spoken almost every day since meeting. He would call. I'd text. But I learned he hated texting. He might send one text, two at most. If the conversation went any further, he would call. He likes talking and listening. He appreciates discourse.

It was weird to be all alone again for those two days when he was away. That was what I'd been used to, before, but after, it felt insufficient. I missed him. I missed being with another person. It's corny, I know, but I felt like a part of me was gone.

Getting to know someone is like putting a never-ending puzzle together. We fit the smallest pieces first and we get to know ourselves better in the process. The details I know about Jake—that he likes his meat well-done, that he avoids using public bathrooms,

that he hates when people pick their teeth with their fingernails after a meal—are trivial and inconsequential compared to the large truths that take time to eventually reveal themselves.

After spending so much time alone, I started to feel like I knew Jake well, really well. If you're seeing someone constantly, like Jake and I did after only two weeks, it starts to feel . . . intense. It was intense. I thought about him all the time those first couple of weeks, even when we weren't together. We'd had lots of long talks while sitting on the floor, or lying on the couch, or in bed. We could talk for hours. One of us starting into a topic, the other picking up on it. We'd ask each other questions. We'd discuss, debate. It wasn't about agreeing all the time. One question would always lead to another. Once, we stayed up all night talking. Jake was different from anyone else I'd ever met. Our bond was unique. Is unique. I still think that.

"Trying to restore a critical balance," Jake says. "That's something we've been thinking about at work lately. Critical balance is needed in everything. I was thinking about this in bed the other night. Everything is so . . . delicate. Take something like metabolic alkalosis—a very slight rise in the pH level of tissue, which has to do with a small dip in hydrogen concentration. It's just . . . it's all extremely subtle. It's only one example, and yet it's vital. There are so many things like this. Everything is impossibly fragile."

"A lot of things are, yeah," I say. Like everything I've been thinking about.

"Some days, a current runs through me. There's an energy in

me. And you. It's something worth being aware of. Does this make any sense? Sorry, I'm rambling."

I have my feet out of my shoes and they're up, resting on the dashboard in front of me. I'm leaning back in my seat. I feel like I could doze off. It's the rhythm of the wheels on the road, the movement. Driving has this anesthetic effect on me.

"What do you mean by the current?" I ask, closing my eyes.

"Just how it feels. You and me," he says. "The singular velocity of flow."

"HAVE YOU EVER BEEN DEPRESSED or anything?" I ask.

We've just made what felt like a significant turn. We'd been on the same road for a while. We turned at a stop sign, not at a light. Left. There are no traffic lights out here.

"Sorry, that was out of the blue. I'm just thinking."

"About what?"

For years, my life has been flat. I'm not sure how else to describe it. I've never admitted it before. I'm not depressed, I don't think. That's not what I'm saying. Just flat, listless. So much has felt accidental, unnecessary, arbitrary. It's been lacking a dimension. Something seems to be missing.

"Sometimes, I feel sad for no apparent reason," I say. "Does this happen to you?"

"Not particularly, I don't think," he says. "I used to worry when I was kid."

"Worry?"

"Yeah, like I would worry about insignificant things. Some people, strangers, might worry me. I had trouble sleeping. I'd get stomachaches."

"How old were you then?"

"Young. Maybe eight, nine. When it would get bad, my mom would make what she called 'kids tea,' which was pretty much all milk and sugar, and we'd sit and talk."

"About what?"

"Usually about what I'd been worried about."

"Do you remember anything specific?"

"I never worried about dying, but I did worry about people in my family dying. Mostly it was abstract fears. For a while I worried one of my limbs might fall off."

"Really?"

"Yeah, we had sheep at our farm, lambs. A day or two after a lamb was born, Dad would put special rubber bands around its tail. They're very tight, enough to stop the blood flow. After a few days, the tail would just fall off. It's not painful for the lambs; they don't even know what's happening.

"Every so often, as a kid, I'd be out in the fields and I'd find a severed lamb tail. I started to wonder if the same thing could happen to me. What if the sleeves on a shirt or a pair of socks were slightly too tight? And what if I slept with my socks on and I woke up in the middle of the night and my foot had fallen off? It made me worry, too, about what's important. Like, why isn't the tail an important part of the lamb? How much of you can fall off before something important is lost? Right?"

"I can see how that might be unnerving."

"Sorry. That was a very long answer to your question. So to answer, I would say that no, I'm not depressed."

"But sad?"

"Sure."

"Why is that—how is that different?"

"Depression is a serious illness. It's physically painful, debilitating. And you can't just decide to get over it in the same way you can't just decide to get over cancer. Sadness is a normal human condition, no different from happiness. You wouldn't think of happiness as an illness. Sadness and happiness need each other. To exist, each relies on the other, is what I mean."

"It seems like more people, if not depressed, are unhappy these days. Would you agree?"

"I'm not sure I'd say that. It does seem like there's more opportunity to reflect on sadness and feelings of inadequacy, and also a pressure to be happy all the time. Which is impossible."

"That's what I mean. We live in a sad time, which doesn't make sense to me. Why is that? Are there more sad people around now than there used to be?"

"There are many around the university, students and profs whose biggest concern each day—and I'm not exaggerating—is how to burn the proper number of calories for their specific body type based on diet and amount of strenuous exercise. Think about that in the context of human history. Talk about sad.

"There's something about modernity and what we value now. Our shift in morality. Is there a general lack of compassion? Of

interest in others? In connections? It's all related. How are we supposed to achieve a feeling of significance and purpose without feeling a link to something bigger than our own lives? The more I think about it, the more it seems happiness and fulfillment rely on the presence of others, even just one other. The same way sadness requires happiness, and vice versa. Alone is . . ."

"I know what you mean," I say.

"There's an old example that gets used in first-year philosophy. It's about context. It goes like this: Todd has a small plant in his room with red leaves. He decides he doesn't like the look of it and wants his plant to look like the other plants in his house. So he very carefully paints each leaf green. After the paint dries, you can't tell that the plant has been painted. It just looks green. Are you with me?"

"Yeah."

"The next day he gets a call from his friend. She's a plant biologist and asks if he has a green plant she can borrow to do some tests on. He says no. The next day, another friend, this time an artist, calls to ask if he has a green plant she can use as a model for a new painting. He says yes. He's asked the same question twice and gives opposite answers, and each time he's being honest."

"I see what you mean."

Another turn, this time at a four-way stop.

"It seems to me that in the context of life and existing and people and relationships and work, being sad is one correct answer. It's truthful. Both are right answers. The more we tell ourselves that we should always be happy, that happiness is an end in

itself, the worse it gets. And by the way, this isn't a very original thought or anything. You know I'm not trying to be brilliant right now, right? We're just talking."

"We're communicating," I say. "We're thinking."

IT'S MY PHONE THAT BREAKS the silence, ringing from my bag. Again.

"Sorry," I say, reaching down to retrieve it. It's my number on the screen. "My friend again."

"Maybe you should answer it this time."

"I really don't feel like talking. She'll stop calling eventually. I'm sure it's nothing."

I put the phone in my bag but pick it up again when it beeps. Two new messages. This time, I'm glad the volume of the radio is high. I don't want Jake to hear the messages. But the Caller's not talking in the first message. It's just sounds, noises, running water. In the second, it's more running water and I can hear him walking, footsteps, and what sounds like hinges, a door closing. It's him. It has to be.

"Anything important?" Jake asks.

"No." I hope to sound casual, but I can feel my face growing warmer.

I'm going to have to deal with this when we get back, tell someone, anyone, about the Caller. But now, if I do say something to Jake, I'll also have to tell him I've been lying. It can't keep going on. Not like this. Not anymore. The running water continues. I'm not sure why he's doing this to me.

"Really? Not important? Two calls, not even texts, in a row. Seems important, no?"

"People are dramatic sometimes," I say. "I'll talk to her tomorrow. My phone's about to die anyway."

I THINK JAKE'S LAST GIRLFRIEND was a grad student in another department. I've seen her around. She's cute: athletic, with blond hair. A runner. He definitely dated her. He says they're still friends. Not close friends. They don't hang out. But he said they had coffee a week before we met at the pub. I probably sound jealous. I'm not. I'm curious. I'm also not a runner.

It's weird, but I'd like to talk to her. I'd like to sit down with a pot of tea and ask her about Jake. I'd like to know why they started dating. What was it about him that attracted her? I'd like to know why it didn't last. Did she end things, or did Jake? If it was her, for how long was she thinking of ending things? Doesn't this seem like a reasonable idea, chatting with a new partner's ex?

I've asked him about her a few times. He's coy. He doesn't say much. He just says their relationship wasn't long or very serious. That's why it's her I have to talk to. To hear her side.

We're alone in a car in the middle of nowhere. Now seems as good a time as any.

"So, how did it end?" I say. "With your last girlfriend, I mean."

"It never really started," he says. "It was minor and temporary."

"But you didn't start out thinking that."

"It didn't start out any more serious than when it ended."

"Why didn't it last?"

"It wasn't real."

"How do you know?"

"You always know," he says.

"But how do we know when a relationship becomes real?"

"Are you asking in general, or about that relationship specifically?"

"That one."

"There was no dependency. Dependency equates to seriousness."

"I'm not sure I agree," I said. "What about real? How do you know when something's real?"

"What *is* real?" he says. "It's real when there are stakes, when something's on the line."

For a while we don't say anything.

"Do you remember me telling you about the woman who lives across the street?" I ask.

I think we must be getting close to the farm. Jake hasn't confirmed we are, but we've been driving for a while. Must be close to two hours.

"Who?"

"The older woman from across the street. Remember?"

"I think so, yeah," he says noncommittally.

"She was saying how she and her husband have stopped sleeping together."

"Hmm."

"I don't mean not having sex. I mean have stopped sleeping in the same bed at night. They both decided a good night's sleep

trumps any benefit to sleeping in the same bed. They want their own sleeping space. They don't want to hear another person snoring or feel them turn over. She said her husband's a pretty vicious snorer."

I find this very sad.

"It seems reasonable that if one person is disruptive, sleeping alone would be an option."

"You think? We spend almost half our lives asleep."

"That could be an argument for why it's best to find the optimal sleeping situation. It's an option, that's all I'm saying."

"But you're not *just* sleeping. You're aware of the other person."

"You *are* just sleeping," he insists.

"You're never just sleeping," I say. "Not even when you're asleep."

"You've lost me."

Jake signals and makes a left turn. This new road is smaller. It's definitely not a main road. This is a back road.

"Aren't you aware of me when we're sleeping?"

"I mean, I don't know. I'm asleep."

"I'm aware of you," I say.

TWO NIGHTS AGO, I COULDN'T sleep. Yet again. I've been thinking too much for weeks. Jake slept over for the third night in a row. I actually like sleeping in bed with someone. Sleeping beside someone. Jake was sound asleep, not snoring, but his breathing was unmistakably close. Right there.

I think what I want is for someone to know me. Really know me. Know me better than anyone else and maybe even me. Isn't that why we commit to another? It's not for sex. If it were for sex, we wouldn't marry one person. We'd just keep finding new partners. We commit for many reasons, I know, but the more I think about it, the more I think long-term relationships are for getting to know someone. I want someone to know me, really know me, almost like that person could get into my head. What would that feel like? To have access, to know what it's like in someone else's head. To rely on someone else, have him rely on you. That's not a biological connection like the one between parents and children. This kind of relationship would be chosen. It would be something cooler, harder to achieve than one built on biology and shared genetics.

I think that's it. Maybe that's how we know when a relationship is real. When someone else previously unconnected to us knows us in a way we never thought or believed possible.

I like that.

In bed that night, I looked over at Jake. He was so stable, babyish. He looked smaller. Stress and tension hide during sleep. He never grinds his teeth. His eyelids don't flutter. He usually sleeps so soundly. He looks like a different person when he sleeps.

During the day, when Jake's awake, there's always an underlying intensity, an energy that simmers. He has these little movements, twitches and ticks.

But isn't being alone closer to the truest version of ourselves, when we're not linked to another, not diluted by their presence and judgments? We form relationships with others, friends,

family. That's fine. Those relationships don't bind the way love does. We can still have lovers, short-term. But only when alone can we focus on ourselves, know ourselves. How can we know ourselves without this solitude? And not just when we sleep.

It's probably not going to work out with Jake. I'm probably going to end it. What's unrealistic, I think, is the number of people who attempt an enduring, committed relationship, who believe it will work long-term. Jake isn't a bad guy. He's perfectly fine. Even considering the data that shows the majority of marriages don't last, people still think marriage is the normal human state. Most people want to get married. Is there anything else that people do in such huge numbers, with such a terrible success rate?

Jake once told me that he keeps a photograph of himself at his desk in his lab. He says it's the only photograph he keeps there. It's of him when he was five. He had curly blond hair and chubby cheeks. How did he ever have chubby cheeks? He told me he likes the photo because it's him, yet physically, he's completely different now from the child he sees in the photo. He doesn't just mean he looks different but that every cell captured in the image has died, been shed and replaced by new cells. In the present, he is literally a different person. Where's the consistency? How is he still aware of being that younger age if he's physically completely different? He would say something about all those proteins.

Our physical structures, like a relationship, change and repeat, tire and wilt, age and deplete. We get sick and better, or sick and worse. We don't know when, or how, or why. We just carry on.

Is it better to be paired up or alone?

Three nights ago, with Jake fully comatose, I waited for the light to start peeking through the blinds. On the nights I can't sleep, like that one, like so many recently, I wish I could just turn my mind off like a lamp. I wish I had a shutdown command like my computer. I hadn't looked at the clock in a while. I lay there, thinking, wishing I was asleep like everyone else.

"Almost there," says Jake. "We're five minutes away."

I sit up and stretch my arms over my head. I yawn. "Felt like a quick trip," I say. "Thanks for inviting me."

"Thanks for coming," he says. Then, inexplicably, "And you also know things are real when they can be lost."

—*The body was found in the closet.*

—*Really?*

—*Yeah. A small closet. Big enough to hang shirts and jackets, some boots, not much else. The body was all scrunched up in there. The door was closed.*

—*It makes me sad. And angry.*

—*Why not reach out to someone, right? Talk to someone. He had coworkers. It wasn't like he was working in a place without other people. There were people around all the time.*

—*I know. It didn't have to happen this way.*

—*Of course not.*

—*Do we know much about his background?*

—*Not a lot. He was smart, well-read. He knew things. He'd had an earlier career, some sort of academic work, PhD level, I think. That didn't last, and he ended up here.*

—*He wasn't married?*

—*No, he wasn't married. No wife. No kids. No one. It's rare these days to see someone living like that, entirely alone.*

It's a long, slow drive up the farm's potholed driveway. Trees line both sides. We bump along for about a minute. The gravel and dirt grind under the tires.

The house at the end of the driveway is made of stone. From here, it doesn't look huge. There's a wooden, railed deck on one side. We park to the right of the house. There are no other vehicles in sight. Don't his parents have a car? I can see a light coming from what Jake says is the kitchen. The rest of the house is dark.

There must be a woodstove inside, because the first thing I smell as soon as I step out of the car is smoke. This would have been a pretty place at one time, I imagine, but now it's a bit run-down. They could use some fresh paint on the windowsills and trim. Much of the porch is rotting. The porch swing is ripped and rusted.

"I don't want to go in yet," says Jake. I've already taken a few steps toward the house. I stop and turn back. "All that sitting in the car. Let's take a walk around first."

"It's a bit dark, isn't it? We can't really see much, can we?"

"At least to get some air, then," he says. "The stars aren't out to-night, but on a clear night in summer they're unbelievable. Three

times as bright as in the city. I used to love that. And the clouds. I remember coming out on humid afternoons and the clouds were so massive and soft-looking. I liked how gently they moved across the sky, how different they were from one another. It's silly, I guess, just watching clouds. I wish we could see them now."

"It's not silly," I say. "Not at all. It's nice that you noticed those things. Most people wouldn't."

"I used to always notice stuff like that. The trees, too. I don't think I do as much anymore. I don't know when that changed. Anyway, you know that it's damn cold when the snow crunches like this. This isn't that wet snowball-making snow," Jake says, walking ahead. I wish he wore gloves; his hands are all red. The interlocking stone path we take from the lane to the barn is uneven and crumbling. I appreciate the fresh air, but it's frigid, not fresh or crisp. My legs are numb. I thought he'd want to go right inside and greet his folks. That's what I was expecting. I'm not wearing warm pants. No long underwear. Jake's giving me what he calls "the abridged tour."

A blustery night is a weird time to be surveying the property. I can tell he really wants me to see it. He points out the apple orchard, and where the veggie gardens are in summer. We come up to an old barn.

"The sheep are in there," he says. "Dad probably gave them some grain an hour ago."

He leads me to a wide door that opens from the top half. We walk in. The light is dim, but I can make out silhouettes. Most of the sheep are lying down. A few are chewing. I can hear it. The

sheep look spiritless, immobilized by the cold, their breath float-
ing up around them. They look at us, vacantly. The barn has thin
plywood walls and cedar pillars. The roof is some type of sheet
metal, aluminum maybe. In several places, the walls are cracked
or contain holes. It seems a dreary place to pass your time.

The barn isn't what I'd pictured. Of course I don't say anything
to Jake. It seems dreary. And it smells.

"That's their cud," says Jake. "They're always doing that. Chewing."

"What's cud?"

"It's semidigested food that they regurgitate and chew like
gum. Beyond the odd bolus sighting, not much excitement in the
barn at this time of night."

Jake doesn't say anything as he leads me out of the barn.
There's something much more disturbing than the cud and the
constant chewing out here. There are the two carcasses up against
the wall. Two woolly carcasses.

Limp and lifeless, both have been stacked up outside against
the side of the barn. It's not what I'm expecting to see. There's no
blood or gore, no flies, no scent, nothing to suggest these were
ever living creatures, no signs of decay. They could just as easily be
made of synthetic rather than organic material.

I want to stare at them, but I also want to get farther away. I've
never seen dead lambs before, other than on my plate with garlic
and rosemary. It seems to me, maybe for the first time, that there
are varying degrees of dead. Like there are varying degrees of everything: of being alive, of being in love, of being committed, of being

sure. These lambs aren't sleepwalking through life. They aren't discouraged or sick. They aren't thinking about giving up. These tailless lambs are dead, extremely dead, ten-out-of-ten dead.

"What will happen to the lambs?" I call to Jake, who's walking ahead, away from the barn. He's hungry now, I can tell, and wants to hurry up, get inside. The wind is picking up.

"What?" he yells over his shoulder. "You mean the dead ones?"

"Yeah."

Jake doesn't reply. He just keeps walking.

I'm not sure what else to say. Why didn't he say anything about the dead lambs? I'm the one who saw them. I'd rather ignore them, but now that I've seen them, I can't.

"Will anything happen to them?" I ask.

"I don't know. What do you mean? They're already dead."

"Do they stay there, or get buried or anything?"

"Probably burn them at some point. In the bonfire. When it gets warmer, in the spring." Jake continues walking ahead of me. "They're frozen for now anyway." They didn't look all that different from lambs that are alive and healthy, at least in my mind. But they're dead. There's something so similar to living, healthy lambs, but also so different.

I jog to catch up, trying not to slip and fall. We're far enough away from the barn now that when I turn back, the shape of the two lambs looks like a single inanimate form, a solid mass—a bag of grain resting against the wall.

"Come on," he calls, "I'll show you the old pen where they used

to keep pigs. They don't have pigs anymore; they were too much work."

I follow him along the path until he stops. The pen looks abandoned, untouched for a few years. That's my feeling. The pigs are gone, but the enclosure is still there.

"So what happened to the pigs?"

"The last two were quite old and weren't moving around much anymore," he says. "They had to be put down."

"And they never got any new ones or baby pigs? Piglets. Is that how it usually works?"

"Sometimes. But I guess they never replaced them. They're a lot of work and expensive to keep."

I should probably know better, but I'm curious. "Why did they have to put the pigs down?"

"That's what happens on a farm. It's not always pleasant."

"Yeah, but were they sick?"

He turns back and looks at me. "Forget it. I don't think you'd like the truth."

"Just tell me. I need to know."

"Sometimes it's hard, out here on a farm like this. It's work. My parents hadn't been inside the pen to check on the pigs for a few days. They just tossed their food into the pen. The pigs were lying in the same corner day after day, and after a while, Dad decided he'd better have a good look at them. When he went inside, the pigs didn't look well. He could tell they were in some discomfort.

"He decided he better try to move them. Dad almost fell over backward when he lifted up the first pig. But he did it. He lifted and turned it. He found its belly was swarming with maggots. Thousands of them. It looked like its entire underside was covered in moving rice. The other one was even worse than the first. Both pigs were literally being eaten alive. From the inside out. And you'd never really know if you just looked at them from afar. From a distance, they seemed content, relaxed. Up close, it was a different story. I told you: life isn't always pleasant."

"Holy shit."

"The pigs were old and their immune systems were probably shot. Infection set in. Rot. They're pigs, after all. They live in filth. It probably started with a small cut on one of them, and some flies landed in the wound. Anyway, Dad had to put the pigs down. That was his only choice."

Jake steers us out and starts walking again, crunching through the snow. I'm trying to use his same footsteps, where the snow's been compressed a bit.

"Those poor creatures," I say. But I get it. I do. They had to be put down and put out of their misery. Suffering like that is unendurable. Even if the solution is final. The two lambs. The pigs. It really is nonnegotiable, I think. There's no going back. Maybe they were lucky, to go like that after what they'd been through. To at least be liberated from some of the suffering.

Unlike the frozen lambs, there's nothing restful or humane about the image of those pigs Jake has planted in my mind. It makes me wonder: What if suffering doesn't end with death? How

can we know? What if it doesn't get better? What if death isn't an escape? What if the maggots continue to feed and feed and feed and continue to be felt? This possibility scares me.

"You have to see the hens," says Jake.

We approach a coop. Jake unlatches the entrance and we duck inside. The chickens are already roosting, so we don't stay in there long. Just long enough for me to step in some runny, unfrozen shit, of course, and to smell the unpleasant smells and see one of the last non-roosting hens eating one of its own eggs. It's not just the barn—every area has a distinct smell. I find it eerie in here with all these chickens sitting up on thin rails, looking at us. They appear more disgruntled by our presence than the sheep were.

"They'll do that sometimes, eat them, if the eggs aren't collected," says Jake.

"Gross," is all I can think of to say. "You guys don't have any neighbors, do you?"

"Not really. Depends on your definition of *neighbor*."

We leave the coop, and I'm grateful to get that smell out of my nose.

We walk around behind the house, my chin pressed down against my chest for warmth. We're off the path now and are making our own way in the unshoveled snow. I don't normally feel so hungry. I'm famished. I look up and see someone in the house, in the upstairs window. A gaunt figure, standing, looking down at us. A woman with long straight hair. The tip of my nose is frozen.

"Is that your mom?" I wave. No response.

"She probably can't see you. Too dark out here."

She stays at the window as we keep walking, plodding through the ankle-deep snow.

MY FEET AND HANDS ARE numb. My cheeks red. I'm glad to be inside. I'm blowing on my hands, thawing them out as we step through the door into a small foyer. I can smell supper. Some kind of meat. There's also that smell of burning wood again, and a distinct atmospheric scent that every house has. Its own smell that its inhabitants are never aware of.

Jake yells hello. His dad—it must be his dad—answers that they'll be down in a minute. Jake seems a bit distracted, almost antsy.

"Do you want some slippers?" he asks. "They might be a bit big for you, but these old floors are pretty cold."

"Sure," I say. "Thanks."

Jake rummages through a wooden bin to the left of the door, filled with hats and scarves, and digs up a pair of worn blue slippers.

"My old ones," he says. "I knew they were in there. What they lack in appearance, they make up for in comfort."

He holds them in both hands, examining them. It's like he's cradling them.

"I love these slippers," he says, more to himself than to me. He sighs and hands me the slippers.

"Thanks," I say, not sure that I should put them on. Eventually, I do. They don't fit right.

"Okay, this way," says Jake.

We step beyond the threshold, to the left, into a small sitting room. It's dark, and Jake twists the switches on some lamps as we move.

"What are your folks doing?"

"They'll be down."

We step into a large room. A living room. The house, unlike outside, is closer to what I'd been expecting. Hand-me-down furniture, rugs, lots of wooden tables and chairs. Each piece of furniture or trinket is distinct. And the decor—not to be so judgmental—but few things match. And everything is antique-looking. There's nothing in here that's been bought in the last twenty years. I guess that can be charming. It feels like we've stepped back in time several decades.

The music adds to this sensation of time travel. Hank Williams, I think. Or Bill Monroe. Maybe Johnny Cash? It sounds like vinyl, but I can't see where it's coming from.

"The bedrooms are upstairs," Jake says, pointing to a staircase outside the living room. "Not much else up there. I can show you after we eat. I told you it's not fancy. It's an old place."

True. Everything is old, but it's remarkably neat, tidy. There's no dust on the side tables. The cushions aren't stained or torn. What old farmhouse doesn't have some dust? No lint or animal hair or threads or dirt on the couch and chairs. The walls are covered in paintings and sketches, lots of them. Most aren't framed. The paintings are large. The sketches vary in size, but most are smaller. There's no TV in this room, or a computer. Lots of lamps. And candles. Jake lights the ones that aren't lit.

I assume it's his mom who collects the ornamental figurines. Most are small children dressed in elaborate attire, hats, and boots. Porcelain, I think. Some of the figurines are picking flowers. Some are carrying hay. Whatever they're doing, they're doing it for eternity.

The woodstove crackles in the far corner. I walk over and stand in front of it, turning to feel its warmth on my back. "Love the fire," I say. "Cozy on a cold night."

Jake sits down on the maroon couch opposite.

A thought occurs to me, and before I can mull it over I blurt it out. "Your parents knew we were coming, right? They invited us?"

"Yeah. We communicate."

Beyond the entrance to this room, past the staircase, is a scratched-up, ragged door. It's closed. "What's in there?"

Jake looks at me as if I've asked a really stupid question. "Just some more rooms. And the basement is through there."

"Oh, okay," I say.

"It isn't finished. Just a nasty hole in the ground for the water heater and stuff like that. We don't use it. It's a waste of space. There's nothing down there."

"A hole in the ground?"

"Just forget about it. It's there. It's not a nice place. That's all. It's nothing."

I hear a door close somewhere upstairs. I look at Jake to see if he registers it, but he's lost in his own mind, looking straight ahead, intently, though seemingly at nothing.

"What are the scratches on the door from?"

"From when we had a dog."

I drift from the stove to the wall of paintings and sketches. I see there are several photographs on the wall, too. All the photos are black-and-white. Unlike the sketches, all the photos are framed. No one is smiling in these photos. Everyone is stern-faced. The photo in the middle is of a young girl, fourteen, maybe younger. She's standing, posed, in a white dress. It's faded.

"Who's this?" I ask, touching the frame.

Jake doesn't stand but looks up from the book he's taken from the coffee table. "My great-grandma. She was born in 1885 or something."

She's skinny and pale. She looks shy.

"She wasn't a happy person. She had issues."

I'm surprised by his tone. It carries an edge of uncharacteristic annoyance.

"Maybe she had a tough life?" I offer.

"Her problems were hard on everyone. It doesn't matter. I don't even know why we keep that photo up. It's a sad story."

I want to ask more about her but don't.

"Who's this?" It's a child, a toddler, maybe three or four.

"You don't know?"

"No. How would I know?"

"It's me."

I lean closer to get a better look. "What? No way. That can't be you. The photo is too old."

"That's just because it's black-and-white. It's me."

I'm not sure I believe him. The child is barefoot and standing on a dirt road beside a tricycle. The child has long hair and is glaring at the camera. I look even closer and feel a twinge in my stomach. It doesn't look like Jake. Not at all. It looks like a little girl. More precise: it looks like me.

—*They say he'd pretty much stopped talking.*

—*Stopped talking?*

—*Became nonverbal. Would work but not talk. It was awkward for everyone. I would pass him in the hall, would say hi, and he'd have a hard time looking at me square in the eye. He'd blush, become distant.*

—*Really?*

—*Yeah, I remember regretting hiring him. And not because he was incompetent. Everything was always clean and tidy. He did his job. But it got to the point where I had this feeling, you know? I sensed something. Like he wasn't quite normal.*

—*This sort of justifies your feeling.*

—*It does. I should have acted, done something, I guess, based on my gut.*

—*You can't start second-guessing after the fact. We can't let the actions of one man make us feel guilty. This isn't about us. We're the normal ones. It's only about him.*

—*You're right. It's good to be reminded of that.*

—*So what now?*

—*We try to forget this, all of it. We find a replacement. We move on.*

At the table now, the smells are very good, thankfully. We skipped lunch today in preparation for this meal. I wanted to ensure I'd be hungry, and I am. My only concerns: my headache and the vague metallic taste in my mouth I've been noticing the last few days. It happens when I eat certain foods, and seems to be the worst with fruit and veggies. A chemical flavor. I have no idea what causes it. When I've noticed it, it's turned me off whatever I'm eating, and I'm hoping it doesn't happen now.

I'm also surprised we haven't met Jake's parents. Where are they? The table is set. The food's here. I can hear shuffling in another room, probably the kitchen. I help myself to a dinner roll, a warm dinner roll, rip it in half and smear a knob of butter across it. I stop myself from eating, realizing I'm the only one who's started. Jake's just sitting there. I'm ravenous.

I'm about to ask Jake about his parents again when the door to the entryway opens and they walk into the room, one behind the other.

I stand up to say hello.

"Sit, sit," says his dad, motioning with his hand. "Nice to meet you."

"Thanks for inviting me. The food smells great."

"I hope you're hungry," says Jake's mom, seating herself. "We're glad you're here."

It happens quickly. No formal introductions. No handshakes. Now we're all here, at the table. I guess this is normal. I'm curious about Jake's parents. I can tell his dad's reserved, borderline stand-offish. His mom is smiling a lot. She hasn't stopped since she appeared from the kitchen. Neither of Jake's parents reminds me of Jake. Not physically. His mom is more made-up than I would have guessed. She's wearing so much makeup I find it sort of unsettling. I would never say that to Jake. Her hair is dyed an inky black. It's glaring against her powdered-white complexion and varnished red lips. She also seems a bit shaky, or delicate, as if she might at any moment shatter like a dropped glass.

She's dressed in an outdated, short-sleeved blue velvet dress with frilly white lace around the neck and sleeves, as if she's just been or is going to a formal reception. Not a kind of dress I see often. It's out of season, more summery than wintry, and too fancy for a simple dinner. I feel underdressed. Also, her feet are bare. No shoes or socks or slippers. When I tucked a napkin into my lap, I caught a glimpse under the table: the big toe of her right foot is missing the nail. Her other toenails are painted red.

Jake's dad is wearing socks and leather slippers, blue work-style pants, and a plaid shirt with the sleeves rolled up. His glasses hang from around his neck on a string. He has a thin Band-Aid on his forehead, just above his left eye.

Food is passed around. We start eating.

"I've been having problems with my ears," Jake's mom announces. I look up from my plate. She's looking right at me, smiling broadly. I can hear the ticking of the tall grandfather clock against the wall behind the table.

"You have more than a problem," Jake's dad responds.

"Tinnitus," she says, putting her hand on her husband's. "It is what it is."

I look at Jake and then back at his mom. "Sorry," I say. "Tinnitus. What is that?"

"It's not very fun," says Jake's father. "No fun at all."

"No, it's not," says his mom. "I hear a buzzing in my ears. In my head. Not all of the time, but a lot of the time. A steady buzzing in the background of life. At first they thought it was just from earwax. But it's not."

"That's terrible," I say, glancing at Jake again. No reaction. He continues to shovel food into his mouth. "I think I've heard of this before," I say.

"And my hearing is generally getting worse. It's all related."

"She asks me to repeat myself *all* the time," his dad says. He sips his wine. I sip mine, too.

"And it's the voices. I hear whispers."

Another wide grin. Again I look at Jake, harder this time. I'm searching his face for answers, but I get nothing. He needs to step in here, help me. But he doesn't.

And it's right then, when I'm looking at Jake for some kind of help, that my phone starts ringing. Jake's mom jumps in her chair.

I can feel my face growing warmer. This isn't good. My phone is in my purse, which is down beside my chair.

Finally. Jake looks up at me. "Sorry, that's my phone. I thought it was dead," I say.

"Your friend again? She's been calling all night."

"Maybe you should answer that," says Jake's mom. "We don't mind. If your friend needs something."

"No, no. It's nothing important."

"Maybe it is," she says.

The phone keeps ringing. No one speaks. After a few rings, it stops.

"Anyway," says Jake's dad, "these symptoms sound worse than they really are." He reaches over, touching his wife's hand again. "It's not like what you see in the movies."

I hear the beep that indicates a message has been left. Another one. I don't want to listen to the message. But I know I'll have to. I can't ignore this forever.

"The Whispers, as I call them," Jake's mom says, "they aren't really voices like yours or mine. They don't say anything intelligible."

"It's tough on her, especially at night."

"Night is the worst," she says. "I don't sleep much anymore."

"And when she does, it's not very restful. For any of us."

I'm sort of grasping at straws here. I'm not sure what to say. "That's really tough. The more research done about sleep, the more we realize how important it is."

My phone starts ringing again. I know it can't be, but it sounds louder this time.

"Seriously? You better answer that," says Jake. He rubs his forehead.

His parents don't say anything, but exchange a glance.

I'm not going to answer it. I can't.

"I'm really sorry," I say. "This is annoying for everyone."

Jake is staring at me.

"Those things can be more trouble than they're worth at times," says Jake's dad.

"Sleep paralysis," says his mother. "It's a serious condition. Debilitating."

"Have you heard of it?" his dad asks me.

"I think so," I say.

"I can't move, but I'm awake. I'm conscious."

His father is suddenly animated, gesturing with his fork as he speaks. "Sometimes I'll wake up in the middle of the night for no reason. I turn over and look at her. She's lying there beside me, on her back, perfectly still, her eyes—they're wide-open and she looks terrified. That always scares me. I'll never get used to it." He stabs at the food on his plate and chews a mouthful.

"I feel a heavy weight. On my chest," Jake's mom says. "It's often hard to breathe."

My phone beeps again. This time it's a long message. I can tell. Jake drops his fork. We all turn to him.

"Sorry," he says. Then there's quiet. I have never seen Jake so singularly focused on his plate of food. He stares at it, but he's stopped eating.

Is it my phone that has put him out? Or did I say something that bothered him? He seems different since we've arrived. His mood. It's as if I'm sitting here alone.

"So how was the drive?" his father asks, prompting Jake to speak, finally.

"It was fine. Busy at first, but after about half an hour or so, the roads calmed right down."

"These country roads don't get a lot of use."

Jake is similar to his parents in ways beyond appearance. Subtle movements. Gestures. Like them, he runs his hands together when thinking. He converses like them, too. A sudden redirection of the discussion away from topics he doesn't want to discuss. It's striking. Seeing someone with their parents is a tangible reminder that we're all composites.

"People don't like driving in the cold and snow, and I don't blame them," Jake's mother says. "There's nothing around here. Not for miles. The empty roads make for relaxing trips, though, don't they? Especially at night."

"And with the new highway, none of these back roads ever get used anymore. You could walk home down the middle and not get run over."

"Might take a while and be a bit cold." His mother laughs, though I'm not sure why. "But you'd be safe."

"I'm so used to fighting traffic," I say. "The drive here was nice. I haven't spent a lot of time in the country."

"You're from the suburbs, right?"

"Born and raised. About an hour or so outside the big city."

"Yes, we've been to your part of the world. It's right near the water?"

"Yes."

"I don't think we've ever been there," she says. I don't know how to reply. Isn't that a contradiction? She yawns, tired by the memory of past travels or the lack of them.

"I'm surprised you don't remember the last time we were there," Jake's dad says.

"I remember lots of things," Jake's mom says. "Jake was here before. With his last girlfriend." She winks at me, or it's something in the wink genus. I just can't tell whether it's a tick or deliberate.

"Don't you remember, Jake? All that food we ate?"

"It's not memorable," Jake replies.

He is finished with his meal. His plate is fully cleaned. I'm not half done with my own. I turn my attention to my food, cutting a piece of rare meat. It's dark and crusty on the outside, rare, pink, and oozy on the inside. There are traces of juice and blood on my plate. There's some jellied salad I haven't touched. My hunger has diminished. I mash some potato and carrot onto a morsel of meat and put it into my mouth.

"It's so nice to have you here with us," says Jake's mom. "Jake never brings his girlfriends around. This is really great."

"Absolutely," says his father. "It's too quiet around here when we're alone, and—"

"I have an idea," says Jake's mother. "It'll be fun."

We all look at her.

"We used to play games a lot. To pass the time. There was one that was my favorite. And I think you'd be great at it. If you're up for it. Why don't you do Jake?" she says to me.

"Yes. Right," Jake's dad answers. "Good idea."

Jake looks at me and then back down. He's holding his fork over his empty plate.

"So, are we going to . . . do you mean, impersonate Jake?" I ask. "Is that the game?"

"Yes," says his mom. "Do his voice, talk like him, do whatever like him. Oh, that would be fun."

Jake's father puts down his cutlery. "This is such a good game."

"I'm not— It's just— I'm not very good at that kind of thing."

"Do his voice. Just for a laugh," his mother insists.

I look at Jake. He won't make eye contact. "Okay," I say, stalling. I don't feel comfortable trying to imitate him in front of his parents, but I don't want to disappoint them.

They are waiting. Staring at me.

I clear my throat. "Hello, I'm Jake," I say, deepening my voice. "Biochemistry has many virtues; so, too, do literature and philosophy."

His father smiles and nods. His mother grins from ear to ear. I'm embarrassed. I don't want to play this game.

"Not bad," says his dad. "Not bad at all."

"I knew she'd be good," says his mom. "She knows him. Inside and out."

Jake looks up. "I'll go," he says.

It's the first thing he's said in a while. Jake doesn't like games.

"That's the spirit," says his mother, clapping.

Jake starts talking in what is clearly meant to be my voice. It's slightly higher pitched than his own, but not comically high. He's not mocking me; he's mimicking me. He's using subtle but accurate hand and facial gestures, brushing invisible hair behind an ear. It's startling, accurate, off-putting. Unpleasant. This isn't a gag impersonation. He's taking this seriously, too seriously. He's becoming me in front of everyone.

I look over at his mom and dad. They are wide-eyed, enjoying the performance. When Jake finishes, there's a pause before his dad bursts out laughing. His mom buckles over, too. Jake's not laughing.

And then a phone rings. For once it's not my phone, though. It's the farm's landline, ringing sharply from another room.

"I better get that," says his mother after the third ring, chuckling as she walks away.

His father picks up his fork and knife and starts eating again. I don't feel hungry anymore. Jake asks me to pass the salad. I do, and he doesn't say thank you.

His mom returns to the room. "Who was it?" Jake asks.

"No one," she says, sitting down. "Wrong number."

She shakes her head and stabs a carrot medallion with her fork.

"You should check your phone," she says. I feel a twinge of something as she eyes me. "Really, we don't mind."

· · ·

I CAN'T EAT DESSERT. NOT only because I'm full. There was an awkward minute when the dessert was brought out, a sort of chocolate log cake with layers of whipped cream. I'd asked Jake to remind his parents that I'm lactose intolerant. He must have forgotten. I can't touch that cake.

While Jake and his parents were in the kitchen, I checked my phone. It's dead. Probably for the best. I'll deal with it in the morning.

When Jake's mom returns to the table, she's wearing a different dress. No one else seems to notice. Maybe she does this all the time? Changing outfits for dessert? It's a subtle change. It's the same style of dress but a different color. Like a computer glitch caused a small distortion to the dress. Maybe she spilled something on the other one? She's also put a Band-Aid on the big toe that has no nail.

"Can we get you something else?" Jake's father asks again. "Are you sure you won't have some cake?"

"No, no. I'm fine, really. Dinner was amazing, and I'm stuffed."

"It's too bad you don't like cream," says Jake's mom. "I know it's a little fattening. But it's tasty."

"It does look good," I say. I hold off correcting her about "not liking it." It has nothing to do with liking it.

Jake hasn't eaten his dessert. He hasn't touched his fork or his plate. He's resting back in his chair, playing with a strand of hair at the back of his head.

I feel a jolt, like I've been pinched, and realize, in shock, that I'm biting my nails. My index finger is in my mouth. I look at my hand. The nail on my thumb is almost half chewed off. When did I

start this? I can't recall, yet I must have been doing this all through dinner. I pull my hand back down to my side.

Is that why Jake was looking at me? How could I not have realized I was chewing my nails like that? I can feel a piece of nail in my mouth, stuck between my molars. Gross.

"Can you take the compost out for me tonight, Jake?" his mother asks. "Your dad's back is still sore, and the bin is full."

"Sure," Jake replies.

Maybe it's just me, but it feels like this whole meal has been a little weird. The house, his parents, the whole trip isn't what I thought it would be. It hasn't been fun or interesting. I didn't think everything would be so old, outdated. It's been uncomfortable since we arrived. His parents are fine—his dad especially—but neither is a great conversationalist. They've talked a lot, mostly about themselves. There's also been some really long stretches of silence, cutlery scraping against plates, the music, the ticking clock, the fire popping.

Because Jake is such a good conversationalist, one of the best I've ever met, I thought his parents would be, too. I thought we'd talk about work and maybe even politics, philosophy, art, things like that. I thought the house would be bigger and in better shape. I thought there would be more live animals.

I remember Jake once telling me that the two most important things for quality intellectual interaction are:

One: keep simple things simple and complex things complex.

Two: don't enter any conversation with a strategy or a solution.

"Excuse me," I say. "I'm just going to pop into the bathroom. Is it just through the door?" My tongue is flicking at the piece of nail in my teeth.

"That's right," says Jake's dad. "Like everything here, it's just that way, at the end of the long hall."

IT TAKES A SECOND OR two to find the light switch in the pitch black, running my hand along the wall. When I flick it on, a resonant buzz sings along with the bright white light. This isn't the normal yellow light I'm used to in bathrooms. It's white in an antiseptic, surgical way that forces me to squint. I'm not sure which is more jarring, the light or the buzz.

I'm much more aware of how dark the house is now that I'm in here with this light.

The first thing I do once I close the door is dislodge the chunk of nail from my teeth and spit it into my hand. It's big. Huge. Disgusting. I drop it into the toilet. I look at my hands. The nail on my ring finger, like the one on my thumb, has been bitten down significantly. There's blood around the edge where the skin and nail meet.

There's no mirror in the vanity above the sink. I wouldn't want to see myself anyway, not today. I feel like I have bags under my eyes. I'm sure I do. I don't feel like myself. Flushed, irritable. I'm feeling the lack of sleep over the last few days and the wine from dinner. The glasses were big. And Jake's dad filled them repeatedly. I've had to pee for half an hour. I sit down on the toilet and feel better. I don't want to go back out, not just yet. My head is still achy.

After dessert, Jake's parents jumped up, cleared the table, and headed to the kitchen, leaving Jake and me alone. We sat without talking much. I could hear his parents in the kitchen. Well, I didn't hear them, not precisely. I couldn't make out words, but I could hear their tone. They were arguing. It seemed something was boiling over from our dinner conversation. It was a heated argument. I'm glad it didn't happen in front of me. Or Jake, for that matter.

"What's going on in there?" I asked Jake, in a whisper.

"In where?"

I flush the toilet and stand. I'm still not quite ready to go back out there. I survey the details around me. There's a tub and a shower. The rings are on the shower pole, but there's no shower curtain. There's a small wastebasket. And a sink. That seems to be it. It's all very neat, very clean.

The white tiles on the walls are the same color as the white floor. I try the vanity mirror. Or where the mirror should be. It opens. Besides one empty prescription pill bottle, the shelves inside are bare. I close the vanity door. The light is so bright.

I wash my hands in the sink and notice a small, dazed housefly on the edge of the basin. Most flies fly away when your hand goes near them. I wave my hand. Nothing. I lightly brush the insect's wing with my finger. It moves slightly but doesn't attempt to fly.

If it can't fly anymore, there's no way it's getting out. It can't climb out. It's stuck in there. Does it understand? Of course not. I use my thumb and crush it against the side of the bowl. I'm not sure why. Not something I normally do. I guess I'm helping it. This way is fast. It seems better than the alternative, whirling the thing

down the drain in a slow, spiraling death. Or just leaving it in the sink. It's just one of so many others.

I'm still looking at the squished fly when I get a feeling that someone has followed me to the bathroom. That I'm not alone. There's no noise outside the door. No knock. I didn't hear any footsteps. It's just a feeling. But it's strong. I think someone's right outside the door. Are they listening?

I don't move. I don't hear anything. I step closer to the door and slowly put my hand on the door handle. I wait another moment, the handle in my hand, and then I fling the door open. There's no one there. Only my slippers, which I left outside before entering. I'm not sure why.

I should say Jake's slippers. The ones he lent me. I thought I'd left them facing toward the bathroom. But now they're facing out, toward the hall. I can't be sure. I must have left them like that. It must have been me.

I leave the door open but step back toward the sink. I run the tap to wash the bits of dead fly away. A drop of red blood lands in the sink. And another. I catch sight of my nose upside down in the reflection of the faucet. It's bleeding. I grab a piece of tissue, ball it up, and press it to my face. Why is my nose bleeding?

I haven't had a nosebleed in years.

I LEAVE THE BATHROOM AND head down the hall. I pass a door that must be for the basement. It's open. A narrow, steep staircase leads down. I stop and put my hand against the open door. The slightest

movement, in either direction, causes it to creak. The hinges need grease. On the landing is a small frayed carpet leading to the wooden steps.

From the kitchen, I hear the sound of dishes being washed and conversation. Jake is in there with his parents. I don't feel the need to rush back. I'll give him some time alone with them.

I can't see much from the top of the stairs. It's dark down there. I can hear something coming from the basement, though. I walk forward. I see a white string hanging to my right as I pass through the door. I pull it and a single bulb buzzes on. I hear the sound from below more clearly now. A dull creak, sharper, higher pitched than the hinges. A hushed, whiny, repetitive grind.

I'm curious to see the basement. Jake said his parents don't use it. So what's down there? What's making that sound? The water heater?

The stairs are uneven and precarious. There's no banister. I see a trapdoor made of floorboards is held open on the right side with a metal clip. The stairs would be hidden under the trapdoor when it's closed. There are scratches, like the scratches on the door in the living room, all over the trapdoor. I run my fingers over them. They aren't very deep. But they look frantic.

I start down. I feel like I'm entering a sailboat's lower deck. Without a banister, I use the wall as a guide.

At the bottom I step onto a large slab of concrete. It's atop the gravel floor. There isn't much room down here. The beamed ceiling is low. Ahead of me are several shelves holding brown cardboard boxes. Old, damp, stained, and fragile. Lots of dust, dirt.

Rows and rows of boxes on shelves. There's so much locked away down here, under the trapdoor. Buried. "We don't use it" is what Jake said. "There's nothing down there." Not totally true. Not true at all.

I turn around. Behind me, past the stairs, I see the furnace, a hot water tank, and an electrical panel. There's something else, a piece of equipment. It's old, rusty, not operational. I'm not sure what it is or was.

This room really *is* little more than a hole in the ground. Probably normal for such an old farmhouse. I imagine it floods in spring. The walls are made of dirt and large hunks of bedrock. They aren't really walls the same way the floor isn't really a floor. No bar or pool table. No table tennis. A few seconds here alone would terrify any kid. There's a smell, too. I don't know what it is. Dank. Uncirculated air. Mold. Rot. What am I doing down here?

I'm about to head back up when, at the far end of the room, just beyond the water tank, I notice what is making the sound. A small white oscillating fan sitting on a shelf. It's so dark I can barely see it. I should really get back upstairs, back to the table.

I don't think Jake wants me to see this. The thought only makes me want to stay here longer, though. I won't take long. I carefully step off the slab and toward the fan. It turns back and forth. Why is there a fan running in winter? It's cold enough as it is.

Near the furnace is a painting on an easel. Is that why the fan is on? To dry the paint? I can't imagine being down here for long stretches, painting. I don't see any paint or brushes. No other art supplies. No chair. Does the painter stand? I'm assuming it's Jake's

mom. But she's taller than I am, and I almost have to bend over so as not to hit my head on the ceiling beams. And why paint all the way down here?

I get closer to the painting. The piece is full of wild, heavy brushstrokes and some very specific detail. It's a portrait of a space, a room. It might be this room, this basement. It is. It's dark, the painting, but I can see the stairs, the concrete slab, the shelves. The only thing that's missing is the furnace. In its place is a woman. Or maybe a man. It's an entity, an individual with long hair. Standing, slightly bent over, with long arms. Long fingernails, really long, almost like claws. They aren't growing longer, sharper. But they look like they are. At the bottom corner of the painting, there's a second person, much smaller; a child?

Staring at this picture, I'm reminded of something Jake mentioned on the drive tonight. I'd been only half listening when he said it, so I'm surprised by how clearly I'm recalling his words now. He talked about why examples are used in philosophy, how most understanding and truth combines certainty, rational deduction, but also abstraction. "It's the integration of both," he said, "that matters." I was looking out my window at the passing fields, watching the bare trees fly by.

"This integration reflects the way our minds work, the way *we function* and interact; our split between logic, reason, and something else," he said, "something closer to feeling, or spirit. There's a word that will probably make you bristle. But we can't, even the most practical-minded of us, understand the world through rationality, not entirely. We depend on symbols for meaning."

I glanced at him without saying anything.

"And I'm not just talking about the Greeks. This is a pretty common thread, West and East. It's universal."

"When you say symbols, you mean . . . ?"

"Allegory," he said, "elaborate metaphor. We don't just understand or recognize significance and validity through experience. We accept, reject, and discern through symbols. These are as important to our understanding of life, our understanding of existence and what has value, what's worthwhile, as math and science. And I'm saying this as a scientist. It's all part of how we work through things, how we make decisions. See, as I'm saying it I hear how it sounds, which is very obvious and trite, but it's interesting."

I look at the painting again. The plain face of the person. Nondescript. The long nails pointing down, wet, almost dripping. The fan creaks back and forth.

There is a small, dirty bookcase beside the painting. It's full of old papers. Pages and pages. Drawings. I pick one up. The paper is thick. And another. They're all of this room. They're all of the basement. And in each drawing there's a different person in place of the furnace. Some with short hair, some with long. One has horns. Some have breasts, some penises, some both. All have the long nails and a similar knowing, paralyzed expression.

In each picture there's the child, too. Usually in the corner. Sometimes in other places—on the ground, looking up at the larger figure. In one, the child is in the stomach of the woman. In another, the woman has two heads, and one of the heads is the child's.

I hear footsteps upstairs. Delicate, soft. Jake's mother? Why did I assume she does the painting and drawing down here? I hear more footsteps upstairs, heavier.

I can hear someone. Talking. Two people. I can. From where? It's Jake's mom and dad, upstairs. They're arguing again.

Arguing might be too strong, but the conversation is not cordial. It's heated. Something's wrong. They're upset. I need to get closer to the vent. There's a rusty paint can by the far wall. I move it directly under the vent. I stand on it, balancing myself against the wall. They are talking in the kitchen.

"He can't keep doing this."

"It's not sustainable."

"He spent all that time to get there, just to quit? He threw it away. Of course I worry."

"He needs predictability, something steady. He's alone too much."

Are they talking about Jake? I put my hand higher on the wall and rise up on my tiptoes.

"You kept telling him he could do whatever he wanted."

"What was I supposed to say? You can't get by day after day being like that, shy, introverted . . . so . . ."

What's she saying? I can't make it out.

"Needs to get out of his own head, move on."

"He left the lab. That was his decision. He never should have started down that path in the first place. The thing is . . ."

Something here I can't make out.

"Yes, yes. I know he's smart. I know. But it doesn't mean he had to go that route."

". . . A job he can keep. Hold down."

Left the lab? So they are talking about Jake? What do they mean? Jake's still working there. It's getting harder to decipher the words. If I can just get a bit higher, closer.

The paint can tips and I crash against the wall. The voices stop. I freeze.

For a second, I think I hear someone move behind me. I shouldn't be down here. I shouldn't be listening. I turn to look back toward the stairs, but there's no one there. Just the shelves full of boxes, the dim light coming from upstairs. I don't hear the voices anymore, not at all. It's quiet. I'm alone.

An awful feeling of claustrophobia settles over me. What if someone were to close the trapdoor covering the stairs? I would be stuck down here. It would be dark. I'm not sure what I would do. I stand up, not wanting to think about it further, rubbing the knee I banged into the wall.

On my way back up the stairs I notice a lock and latch on the trapdoor, the one that hides the stairs when it's closed. The latch is screwed into the wall beside the stairs, but the lock's on the bottom of the trapdoor. You'd think it would be on the top side, so they could lock it from the top. The trapdoor can be closed and opened from either side, either pushed up if you're in the basement, or pulled up if you're on the landing. But it can be locked only from below.

—*Do we know the official cause of death?*

—*Bled out, from the puncture wounds.*

—*Awful.*

—*Bled for hours, we think. Quite a bit of blood.*

—*It must have been terrible to stumble across.*

—*Yes, I imagine it was. Horrible. Something you'd never forget.*

The dining room is empty when I return from the basement. The table has been cleared except for my dessert plate.

I poke my head into the kitchen. The dirty plates are stacked and rinsed, but not washed. The sink is filled with grayish water. The faucet drips. Drips.

"Jake?" I call. Where is he? Where is everyone? Maybe Jake is taking out the table scraps to the compost in the shed.

I spot the stairs to the second floor. Soft green carpet on the treads. Wood-paneled walls. More photographs. A lot are of the same elderly couple. They're all old photographs, none of Jake when he was younger.

Jake told me he would show me the upper floor after dinner, so why not go check it out now? I head straight to the top, where there's a window. I look out, but it's too dark to see outside.

On my left is a door with a small stylized *J* hanging from it. Jake's old bedroom. I walk in. I sit down on Jake's bed and look around. Lots of books. Four full cases. Candles on top of each bookcase. The bed is soft. The blanket on top is what I would expect in an old farmhouse—knitted and homemade. It's a small bed for such a tall guy, just a single. I put my hands out beside me,

palms down, and bob up and down, like an apple dropped in water. The springs squeak a bit, showing their age and years of use. Old springs. Old house.

I stand. I walk past a heavily used, comfy-looking blue chair, over to the desk in front of a window. There's not much on the desk. Some pens, pencils in a mug. A brown teapot. A few books. A pair of large silver scissors. I slide open the top drawer of the desk. There's the usual desk stuff in there—paper clips, notepads. There's also a brown envelope. It has *Us* printed on the outside. It looks like Jake's handwriting. I can't just leave it. I pick it up, open it.

Inside are photos. I probably shouldn't be doing this. It's not really my business. I flip through them. There are about twenty or thirty. They're all close-up shots. Body parts. Knees. Elbows. Fingers. Lots of toes. Some lips and teeth, gums. A few extreme close-ups, just hair and skin, pimples maybe. I can't tell if they're all the same person or not. I put them back in the envelope.

I've never seen photos like that. Are they some sort of art thing? Like for a show, or display, or some installation? Jake has mentioned to me that he's into photography and that the only activity he did outside of school was art lessons. He said he has a really nice camera that he saved up for.

There are lots of photos around the room, too, scenes, some of flowers and trees, and people. I don't recognize any of the faces. The only one of Jake I've seen in the house is that one downstairs by the fire, the one he claimed was him when he was a kid. But it wasn't. I'm sure it wasn't. That means I've never seen a photo of Jake. He's shy, I know, but still.

I pick up a framed photo from a shelf. A blond girl. She has a blue bandanna headband, tied in the front. His high school girl-friend? She'd been deeply in love with him, or so Jake claimed, and the relationship had never quite meant the same thing to him as it had to her. I bring the photo up to my face, almost touching my nose. But Jake had said she was a brunette and tall. This woman is blond, like me, and short. Who is she?

In the background I notice someone else. It's a man, not Jake. He's looking at the girl in the photo. He's connected to the woman. He's close and is looking at her. Did Jake take the photo?

I jump as a hand touches my shoulder.

It's not Jake. It's his father. "You startled me," I say.

"Sorry, I thought you were in here with Jake."

I put the photo back on the shelf. It falls to the floor. I bend down and pick it up.

When I turn back to Jake's dad, he's grinning. He has a second Band-Aid on his forehead, above the original one.

"I didn't mean to startle you, I just wasn't sure if you were all right. You were trembling."

"I'm fine. I'm a little cold, I guess. I was waiting for Jake. I hadn't seen his room yet and just thought . . . Was I really trembling?"

"From the back, it looked like it—Just a little."

I don't know what he's talking about. I wasn't shaking. How could I be? Am I cold? Maybe I am. I have been cold since before we sat to eat.

"Are you sure you're okay?"

"Yeah, I am. I'm fine." He's right. I look down and notice my hand is trembling slightly. I bring my hands together behind me.

"He used to spend lots of time in here. We're slowly converting it into a guest room," Jake's father says. "We never felt right putting our guests in here when it was still so reminiscent of a bookworm high schooler. Jake always liked his books and stories. And writing in his diaries. It was a comfort for him. He could work through things that way."

"That's nice. I've noticed he still likes to write. He spends a lot of time writing."

"That's how he makes sense of the world."

I feel something as he says this, compassion for Jake, affection.

"It's quiet in here," I say, "at the back of the house. It would be good for writing."

"Yes, and great for sleeping, too. But Jake, as you probably know, Jake was never a good sleeper. You guys are welcome to stay the night. We hoped you would. You don't need to rush off. I told Jake. We want you to stay. We have plenty of food for the morning. Do you drink coffee?"

"Well, thanks, I should probably leave the decision up to Jake. I do love coffee. But Jake has to work in the morning."

"Does he?" his father says, a puzzled look on his face. "Anyhow, it would be great if you stayed. Even just one night. And we want you to know, we're very grateful that you're here. For what you're doing."

I tuck some stray hairs behind my ear. What am I doing? I'm not sure I understand. "It's nice to be here, and nice to meet you."

"It's good for Jake, all of this. You've been good for him. It's been so long since . . . But, I just think this is good for him, finally. We're hopeful."

"He always talks about the farm."

"He was excited for you to see it. We've been looking forward to having you here for so long. We were starting to think he'd never bring you home, after all this time."

"Yeah," is all I can think to say. "I know." After all *what time*?

Jake's dad checks behind him and then takes a step closer to me. He's close enough that I could reach out and touch him. "She's not crazy, you know. You should know that. I'm sorry about to-night."

"What?"

"My wife, I mean. I know how it must seem. I know what you're thinking. I'm sorry. You think she's going mad or is mentally ill. She's not. It's just a hearing thing. She's been under some stress."

Again, I'm unsure how to respond. "I didn't really think that," I say. In truth, I'm not sure what I think.

"Her mind is still very sharp. I know she mentioned voices, but it's not as dramatic as it sounds. They are small whispers and mumbles, you know. She's having discussions with . . . them. With the whispers. Sometimes it's just breathing. It's innocuous."

"That still must be hard," I say.

"They're considering cochlear implants, if her hearing worsens."

"I can't imagine what that must be like."

"And all that smiling. I know it looks a little odd, but it's just a reaction she has. In the past it would have upset me, but I'm used to it now. Poor thing. Her face starts to hurt from so much smiling. But you get used to these things."

"I didn't notice, or not so much."

"You've been very good for him." He turns toward the door. "You guys are a good match. Not that you need me to tell you. Certain things, like math and music, go together well, don't they?"

I smile, nod. Smile again. I don't know what else to do. "It's been great getting to know Jake, and now meeting you and his mom."

"We all like you. Especially Jakie. It makes sense. He needs you."

I keep smiling. I can't seem to stop.

I'M READY TO GO. I want to get out of here. I have my coat on. Jake's already outside, warming up the car. I'm waiting for his mom. I have to say good-bye, but she's gone back to the kitchen to put a plate of leftovers together for us. I don't want it, but how can I say no? I'm standing here alone, waiting. I'm fiddling with the zipper on my coat. Up and down, up and down. I could have warmed up the car. He could have waited here.

She emerges from the kitchen. "I put a little of everything together," she says, "some cake, too." She hands me a single plate of food, covered in foil. "Try to keep it straight or you'll have a mess on your hands."

"Okay, I will. Thanks again for the lovely evening."

"It was lovely, wasn't it? And you're sure you can't stay overnight? We'd love for you to stay. We have room for you."

She's almost pleading. She's close enough to me now that I can see more of the lines and wrinkles on her face. She looks older. Tired, drawn. It's not the way I'd want to remember her.

"We wanted to stay, but I think Jake needs to get back."

We stand for a moment, and then she leans in to give me a hug. We remain like this, with her squeezing me like she doesn't want to let me go. I find myself doing the same thing back. For the first time tonight, I smell her perfume. Lilies. It's a scent I recognize.

"Wait, I almost forgot," she says. "Don't go just yet."

She releases me from her embrace, turns, and heads back to the kitchen again. Where's Jake's dad? I can smell the food on the plate. It's unappetizing. I hope it won't smell up the whole car for the entire drive home. Maybe we can put it in the trunk.

Jake's mom returns. "I decided tonight that I want you to have this."

She hands me a piece of paper. It's been folded a few times. It's small enough to fit into a pocket.

"Oh, thanks," I say. "Thank you."

"I've forgotten now, of course, how long exactly, but it's been in the works for quite some time."

I start to unfold it. She raises her hand. "No, no. Don't open it here! You're not ready yet!"

"I'm sorry?"

"It's a surprise. For you. Open it when you arrive."

"When I arrive where?"

She doesn't answer, just keeps smiling. Then she says, "It's a painting."

"Thank you. Is it one of yours?"

"Jake and I used to draw and paint together when he was younger, for hours at a time. He loved art."

Did they do that in the dank basement? I wonder.

"We have a studio. It's quiet. It was our favorite room in the house."

"Was?"

"Is. Was. Oh, I don't know, you'd have to ask Jake."

Her eyes have welled up and I'm worried she's going to outright cry.

"Thank you for the gift," I say. "That's so kind of you. We'll both appreciate it, I'm sure. Thanks."

"It's for you. Only for you. It's a portrait," she says. "Of Jake."

WE HAVEN'T REALLY TALKED ABOUT the night. We haven't discussed his parents. I thought it would be the first thing we'd do when we got back in the car, rehash the evening. I want to ask about his mom, the basement, tell him about the conversation with his dad in Jake's bedroom, the way his mom hugged me, the gift she gave me. There's so much I want to ask. But we've been in this car a while now. How long? I'm not sure. And now I'm losing steam. I'm starting to fade. Should I just wait and talk about it all tomorrow when I have more energy?

I'm glad we didn't stay the night. I'm relieved. Would Jake and I have shared that tiny single bed? I didn't dislike his parents. It's just that it was weird and I'm tired and want to be in my own bed tonight. I want to be alone.

I can't imagine making small talk with his parents first thing in the morning. Too much to bear. The house was cold, too, and dark. It felt warm when we first got inside, but the longer we were there, the more I noticed the drafts. I wouldn't have slept much.

"Teardrops are aerodynamic," Jake says. "All cars should be shaped like teardrops."

"What?" It comes out of nowhere, and I'm still thinking about the evening, everything that happened. Jake was quiet most of the night. I still don't know why. Everyone gets a little antsy around family, and it was the first time I'd met them. But still. He was definitely less talkative, less present.

I need to sleep. Two or three nights of long, uninterrupted sleep to catch up. No spinning thoughts, no bad dreams, no phone calls, no interruptions, no nightmares. I've been sleeping terribly for weeks. Maybe longer.

"It's funny to see some of these cars that are still being designed and marketed as fuel-efficient. Look how boxy that one is." Jake points out the window to my right, but in the dark it's hard to see anything.

"I don't mind uniqueness," I say. "Even things that are very unique. I like things that are different."

"By definition, nothing can be *very* unique. It's either unique or it isn't."

"Yeah, yeah, I know." I'm too tired for this.

"And cars shouldn't be unique. That driver probably complains about global warming and climate change and yet wants a 'unique' car. Every car should be shaped like a teardrop. That would show people we're serious about fuel efficiency."

He's off on a Jake rant. I don't really care about fuel efficiency, right now or even at the best of times. All I want to do is talk about what just happened at his parents' house and get home so I can get some sleep.

"WHO WAS THAT GIRL IN the photo on your shelf?"

"What photo? What girl?"

"The girl with blond hair standing in a field or at the edge of a field. The one in your room."

"Steph, I guess. Why do you ask?"

"Just curious. She's pretty."

"She's attractive. I never really saw her as beautiful or anything."

She's very pretty. "Did you date her, or is she a friend?"

"Was a friend. We dated for a bit. Just after high school, for a bit after."

"Was she also in biochemistry?"

"No, music. She was a musician."

"What kind?"

"She played a lot of instruments. Taught. She was the first one to introduce me to some of the old stuff. You know, classics,

Country, Dolly Parton, stuff like that. There were narratives in those songs."

"Do you ever see her?"

"Not really. It didn't work out."

He's not looking at me but straight ahead at the road. He's biting his thumbnail. If this were a different relationship, at a different time, maybe I would keep at him. Nag him more. Insist. But I know where we're headed now, so there's no point.

"Who was the guy in the background?"

"What?"

"In the background, behind her, there was a guy lying on the ground. He was looking at her. It wasn't you."

"I don't know. I'd have to see the photo again."

"You must know the one I mean."

"I haven't looked at those photos in a long time."

"It's the only one with her in it. And it's weird, because this guy . . ." I can't say it. Why can't I say it?

A minute goes by. I think he's going to let it fade, to ignore my question, but then he says, "It's probably my brother. I think I remember him being in one of those pictures."

What? Jake has a brother? How has this not come up before?

"I didn't know you had a brother."

"I thought you knew."

"No! This is crazy. How did I not know this?"

I say it jokingly. But Jake is in serious mode, and I probably shouldn't joke.

"Are you two close?"

"I wouldn't say that."

"Why not?"

"Family stuff. It's complicated. He took after my mom."

"And you don't?"

For a second he glares at me, then looks back to the road. We're alone out here. It's late. We haven't passed many cars since the boxy one. Jake is focused on what lies ahead. Without looking at me he asks, "Does it seem normal to you?"

"What?"

"My house. My parents."

"What do you care about normal?"

"Just answer. I want to know."

"Sure. For the most part, yeah."

I'm not going to get into how I really feel. Not now, not since that was the last time we'll be at the farm together.

"I'm not trying to pry, but okay, you have this brother, and how is he like your mom, exactly?"

I'm not sure how he'll react to the question. I think he was trying to change the subject away from his brother. But I think now's the best time to ask. It's the only time to ask.

Jake's rubbing his forehead with one hand, his other one on the wheel.

"A few years ago, my brother developed some problems. We didn't think it was anything serious. He'd always been extremely solitary. Couldn't relate to others. We thought he was depressed. Then he started following me around. He didn't do anything dangerous, but it was odd, the following. I asked him to stop, but he

didn't. There was not a lot of recourse to take. I kind of had to cut him out of my life, block him out. It's not like he couldn't take care of himself. He can. I don't believe he's seriously mentally ill. Not dangerously. I think he can be rehabilitated. I believe he's a genius and he's deeply unhappy. It's hard to spend that much time alone. It's hard not to have anyone. A person can live like that for a while, but . . . My brother got very sad, very lonely. He needed things, asked for things I couldn't help with. It's not a big deal anymore. But of course it changed the dynamic of our family."

This is big. I feel like I understand his parents better now, and Jake, too, just in the last thirty seconds. I'm onto something, and I'm not prepared to let it go. This might have an influence on me, on us, on the question I've been thinking about. "What do you mean he followed you around?"

"It doesn't matter. He's not around anymore. It's over now."

"But I'm interested."

Jake turns up the radio, just a bit, but considering we're talking, it's annoying.

"My brother was on track to become a full professor but couldn't handle the environment. He had to leave his work. He could do the job, but everything else, anything to do with interacting with coworkers, was too hard on him. He'd start every day with a wave of anxiety at the thought of interacting with people. The strange part is he liked them. He just couldn't handle speaking with them. You know, like normal people. Small talk and that."

I notice Jake has started to accelerate as he talks. I don't think he realizes how fast we're going.

"He needed to make a living but had to find a new job, somewhere he didn't have to give presentations, where he could blend into the walls. Around that time he was in a bad place, and he started following me around, talking to me, giving me orders and ultimatums, like a voice in my head, always there. He was interrupting my life, like a sort of sabotage. Subtle stuff."

"How so?"

Our speed is still picking up.

"He started wearing my clothes."

"Wearing your clothes?"

"Like I said, he has some issues, *had* some issues. I don't think it's a permanent thing. He's better now, all better."

"Were you close? Before he got sick?"

"We were never overly close. But we got along. We're both smart and competitive, so that creates a bond. I don't know. I never saw it coming—his illness, I mean. He just sort of lost it. It can happen. But it makes you wonder about knowing people. He's my brother. But I don't know if I ever really knew him."

"Must be tough. For everyone."

"Yeah."

Jake doesn't seem to be increasing the speed, but we're still going too fast. It's not nice out. And it's dark.

"So is that what your dad was talking about when he said your mom has been stressed?"

"When did he tell you that? Why's he telling you that?"

He steps harder on the gas again. I hear the engine revving this time.

"He saw me in your room. He came in to talk to me. He mentioned your mom's condition. Not in detail, but . . . How fast are we going, Jake?"

"Did he mention trichotillomania?"

"What?"

"How she pulls out her hair. My brother had it, too. She's very self-conscious about it. She's pulled out most of her eyebrows and eyelashes. She's already started on her head. I could see some thinner spots tonight."

"That's terrible."

"My mom's pretty fragile. She'll be fine. I didn't realize it had gotten so bad. I wouldn't have invited you had I known it would be so tense tonight. Somehow, in my head, it wasn't going to be like that. But I wanted you to see where I'm from."

It's the first time since we arrived at the house, the first time all evening, that I feel a bit closer to Jake. He's letting me in on something. I appreciate his honesty. He didn't have to tell me any of this. It's not easy stuff to talk about, to think about. This is the kind of thing, the kind of feeling that complicates everything. Maybe I haven't made up my mind yet, about him, about us, about ending things.

"Families have quirks. All of them."

"Thanks for coming," he says. "Really."

I feel a hand on mine.

—We've talked with almost everyone he'd worked with and have been able to put a picture together. He'd been developing physical problems. Issues. Everyone noticed. He had a rash on his arm and neck. His forehead would get sweaty. Someone saw him a few weeks ago at his desk in a sort of daze, just looking at the wall.

—That all sounds alarming.

—I know it does now. But in the context of then, it seemed private, like his own health issue. No one wanted to meddle. There were a few incidents. Over the last year or so he was playing his music quite loud during his breaks. And when people would ask him to turn it down, he'd just ignore them and start the song over again.

—No one thought to make a formal complaint?

—For playing music? Didn't seem like a big deal.

—I guess not.

—Two people we've interviewed mentioned he had notebooks. He wrote a lot. But no one ever asked about what he was writing.

—No, I suppose not.

—We found those notebooks.

—What was in them?

—His writing.

—*He had very neat, precise penmanship.*
—*But what about the content?*
—*The content of what?*
—*The notebooks. Isn't that what matters? What he was writing about? The content? What it might mean?*
—*Right. Well, we haven't read them yet.*

"**D**o you want to stop for something sweet?"

We were on a mini roll there, conversationally, but I've stopped asking questions. I haven't mentioned Jake's family again. I shouldn't pester him. Maybe privacy is a good thing. I'm still thinking about what he said, though. I felt like I was starting to really understand him, appreciate things he's been through. Sympathize.

I also haven't mentioned my headache again, not since we got in the car. The wine made it worse, maybe. The air in that old house. My whole head is sore. I'm holding it in such a way, with my neck taut and slightly forward, so that the pressure is relieved somewhat, only somewhat. Any movement, bump, or twitch is uncomfortable.

"We could stop, sure," I say.

"But do you want to?"

"I'm indifferent, but happy to if you want to."

"You and your nonanswers."

"What?"

"The only place open this late is Dairy Queen. But they'll definitely have some nondairy stuff." So he does remember. About my intolerance.

It's dark outside the car. We've been talking less on the drive home than on the drive there. Both tired, I guess; introspective. Hard to tell if it's snowing. I think it is. Not heavily, though. Not yet. It's just starting. I laugh, more to myself, and look out the window.

"What?" he asks.

"It's pretty funny. I can't eat dessert at your parents' place because there's dairy in it, and we're stopping to get something to eat at Dairy Queen. And it's the middle of winter. It's freezing out; it's snowing, I think. It's fine; it's just funny." I think it's other things, too, but decide not to say anything.

"I haven't had a Skor Blizzard in ages. I think that's what I'll get," he says. Skor Blizzard. I knew it. So predictable.

We pull in. The lot is empty. There's a pay phone booth in one corner and a metal garbage bin in the other. Don't see too many pay phones anymore. Most have been removed.

"I still have a headache," I say. "Think I'm tired."

"I thought it was better."

"Not really." It's worse. It's bordering on a migraine.

"How bad? Migrainous?"

"It's not too bad."

Outside the car, it's cold, windy. The snow is getting heavier now for sure. More swirling than falling. It's not staying on the ground yet. It will once it gets going. Hopefully I'll be in bed by then, with some Advil. If my headache is gone tomorrow, I'll spend the morning shoveling. The cold feels nice on my head.

"Has the feel of a big storm," says Jake. "Wind is freezing."

Looking into the brightly lit Dairy Queen makes me feel nauseated. Of course the Dairy Queen is empty. You have to wonder why it's even open tonight. I noticed the hours on the door and calculated that they're closing in eight minutes. There is no bell chime or the expected overhead Muzak upon entry. The empty tables are clean, no balled napkins or empty cups or crumbs. The store is prepped for close. The dull, metallic drone from the machines and freezers creates a cumulative noise. It reminds me of a dial tone. There's a scent in here, too, almost chemical. We wait, looking up at the glowing menu.

He's reading the menu. I can tell by his eyes, the way he's touching his chin. "I'm sure they'll have something nondairy," he says again.

Jake's already holding a long, red plastic spoon he grabbed from a bin. It's kind of irritating how he grabbed a spoon for himself and we don't even know if there's anything I can eat. We still have plenty of driving ahead of us. A longer trip if the storm gets worse. Maybe we should have stayed the night at the farm. But I just wasn't totally comfortable. I don't know. Jake yawns.

"Are you good, or do you want me to drive the rest of the way home?" I ask.

"No, no, I'm fine. I had less to drink than you did."

"We had the exact same."

"But it affects you way more. Subjectivity and all that." He yawns again, wider, this time bringing his hand up to his mouth. "Yeah, see, they have different flavors of lemonade. And it's iced, dairy-free lemonade," he says. "You'll like that."

"Like. Sure," I say. "I'll have one."

Two employees have emerged from a back room. They look displeased that we've disturbed them. Youngish, teenagers, both of them. They have different shapes, different body types, but in all other facets are identical. They have the same dyed hair, the same tight black pants, the same brown boots. Both would so clearly rather be anywhere else, and I don't blame them.

"We'll have a small lemonade. And actually make it two lemonades. How big is your medium?" Jake asks.

One of the girls grabs a largish-looking paper cup and holds it up. "Medium," she says, flatly. The other girl turns away and giggles.

"That's fine," he says. "One small, one medium."

"The small should be a strawberry lemonade, please, not just the normal lemonade," I say to the girl. "There's no dairy in that, right?"

The girl asks the other girl: "There's no ice cream in the lemonade, is there?" She is still giggling and has a hard time answering. Now the first girl is laughing, too. They're exchanging glances.

"How bad is the allergy?" asks the second girl.

"It won't kill me. I just wouldn't feel well."

It's almost like they recognize us, and it's weird for them, the same way it would be if a friend of one of their parents came in, or one of their teachers showed up unexpectedly and they had to serve them. That's how they're reacting. I look at Jake. He seems oblivious. The first girl looks at him, then whispers something to the second girl. They both laugh again.

A third girl now. She comes from the back. She must have been listening, because without a word she starts to make my lemonade. The other girls don't say anything to her, either, or acknowledge her presence.

The third girl looks up from the machine. "Sorry for the smell," she says. "They're doing some varnishing in the back."

Varnishing? In a Dairy Queen? "No worries," I say.

It's a sudden feeling, but unmistakable. I know this girl. I recognize her but have no idea from where or when. Her face, her hair. Her build. I know her.

She doesn't say anything else. She just sets to work making the lemonade. Or she preps the cups, anyway. She pushes some buttons, turns some knobs. She stands in front of the machine like she's waiting in line at a store. As the machine does the work, the girl holds her hand on one of the empty cups underneath, waiting for the machine to dispense the fluid.

This has never happened to me before, recognizing a perfect stranger. I can't say anything to Jake. It would sound too weird. It *is* weird.

She's skinny and frail, this girl. Something's not right. I feel bad for her. Her dark hair is long and plain and falls over her back and much of her face. Her hands are small. She's not wearing any jewelry, no necklace or rings. She appears fragile and anxious. She has a rash. A bad one.

Starting an inch or so above her wrist are raised bumps, just large enough for me to see. They get worse, redder, up her elbow. I'm looking intensely at her rash. It looks sore and itchy. It's dry, too,

and flaky. She must be scratching it. When I look up she's looking at me. Staring. I feel my face blush, divert my eyes to the floor.

Jake isn't paying any attention. I sense that she's still looking at me, though. I hear one of the girls snicker. The skinny one lids the cup and puts it down on the counter. Her hand moves up and her fingers start to scratch her rash. Not aggressively. I don't want to keep looking. She's sort of picking at the bumps, almost trying to dig them out of her arm. There's a tremble, now, in her hand.

The machine whirls on. Of course, none of these girls wants to be here. This antiseptic Dairy Queen with fridges and freezers and fluorescent lighting and metal appliances and red spoons, straws wrapped in plastic, and cup dispensers and the quiet but constant buzz overhead.

It would be even harder if two of your coworkers were picking on you. Is that why the skinny girl seems distraught?

It's not just this Dairy Queen—it's this place, this town, if it is a town. I'm unclear what makes a town a town, or when a town becomes a city. Maybe this isn't either. It feels lost, detached. Hidden from the world. I'd go moldy out here if I couldn't leave, if there was nowhere else to go.

Somewhere inside the silver machine, ice is being crushed and blended with concentrated lemon juice and lots of liquid sugar. No dairy, but it'll be sweet, I'm sure of that.

The icy lemonade flows out of the machine into the second cup. When it's full, the machine stops, and the girl puts a plastic cover on it, too. She carries them over to where I'm standing. Up close, she looks even worse. It's her eyes.

"Thanks," I say, reaching for the lemonade. I'm not expecting an answer, so I am taken aback when she speaks.

"I'm worried," she mumbles, more to herself than me. I look around to see if the other girls hear her. They aren't paying attention. Neither is Jake.

"Excuse me?"

She's looking down at the floor. She's holding her hands in front of her.

"I shouldn't be saying this, I know I shouldn't. I know what happens. I'm scared. I know. It's not good. It's bad."

"Are you okay?"

"You don't have to go."

I can feel my pulse skipping ahead. Jake is getting straws, I think, and napkins from the dispenser. We won't need spoons after all.

One of the girls laughs, louder this time. The skinny girl in front of me is still looking down, hair covering her face.

"What are you scared of?"

"It's not what I'm scared of. It's who I'm scared for."

"Who are you scared for?"

She picks up the cups. "For you," she says, handing me the cups before disappearing back into the kitchen.

JAKE IS OBLIVIOUS, AS USUAL. We get back to the car, and he doesn't mention anything about the girls in the Dairy Queen. At times he can be very unaware, very self-obsessed.

"Did you see that girl?"

"Which one?"

"The one who made the lemonades?"

"There were several girls."

"No, only one girl made the drinks. Skinny. Long hair."

"I don't know," he says. "I don't know. Weren't they all skinny?"

I want to say more. I want to talk about that girl and her rash and her sad eyes. I want to tell him what she said. I hope she has someone to talk to. I want to understand why she's afraid. It doesn't make sense for her to be afraid for me.

"How's your drink?" Jake asks. "Too sweet?"

"It's okay. Not too sweet."

"That's why I don't like getting those iced drinks, the lemonades and slushies, because they're always cloyingly sweet. I should have gotten a Blizzard."

"It must be nice to be able to have ice cream when you want it."

"You know what I'm saying."

I shake the cup in my hand and push the straw down and up, the friction making a squeaking sound. "It's sour, too," I say. "Fake sour, but sour. It evens out the sweet."

Jake's drink is melting in the cup holder. Soon it will be completely liquid. He's drunk about half.

"I always forget how hard these are to finish. I only needed a small. There's nothing medium about the medium."

I lean forward and turn up the heat.

"Cold?" asks Jake.

"Yeah, a little. Probably from the lemonade."

"We're also in a snowstorm. Whose idea was it to get iced drinks, anyway?"

He looks at me and raises his eyebrows.

"I don't know what I was thinking," he says. "I get sick of these after four sips."

"I'm not saying anything," I say, raising both hands. "Not a word."

We both laugh.

This will probably be the last time I'm in a car with Jake. It seems a shame when he's like this, joking, almost happy. Maybe I shouldn't end things. Maybe I should stop thinking about it and just enjoy him. Enjoy us. Enjoy getting to know someone. Why am I putting so much pressure on us? Maybe I will eventually fall in love and lose any fears I have. Maybe it will get better. Maybe that's possible. Maybe that's how it works with time and effort. But if you can't tell the other person what you're thinking, what does that mean?

I think that's a bad sign. What if he was thinking the same things about me right now? What if he was the one thinking about ending things but also was still having fun, or not entirely sick of me yet, so was keeping me around just to see what would happen. If that's what was going on in his head, I'd be upset.

I should end it. I have to.

Whenever I hear the "it's not you, it's me" cliché, it's hard not to laugh. But it really is true in this case. Jake is just Jake. He's a

good person. He's smart and handsome, in his way. If he were an asshole or stupid or mean or ugly or anything, then it would be his fault that I end things, kind of. But he's not any of those things. He's a person. I just don't think the two of us are a match. An ingredient is missing, and, if I'm being honest, it always has been.

So that's probably what I'll say: It's not you, it's me. It's my issue. I'm the one with the problem. I'm putting you in an unfair position. You're a good person. I need to work through some things. You need to move on. We tried, we did. And you never know what'll happen in the future.

"Looks like you're done," says Jake.

I realize I've put my lemonade in the cup holder. It's melting. I am done. Done.

"I'm cold. It's interesting to watch things melt and feel cold."

"That was a bit of a wasted stop." He looks at me. "Sorry."

"At least I can say I've been to a Dairy Queen in the middle of nowhere in a snowstorm. That's something I'll never do again."

"We should get rid of these cups. They'll melt and the cup holders will get sticky."

"Yeah," I say.

"I think I know where we can go."

"You mean to throw them out?"

"If we keep going, up ahead, there's a road on the left. Down that road a bit is a school, a high school. We can get rid of the cups there."

Is it really that important to get rid of these cups? Why would we stop just to do that?

"It's not far, is it?" I ask. "The snow's not gonna get any better. I'd really like to get home."

"Not too far, I don't think. I just don't want to throw the cups out the window. It'll give you a chance to see a bit more of this area."

I'm not sure if he's joking about "seeing" more of this area. I look out the window. It's just a mix of blowing snow and darkness.

"You know what I mean," he says.

Several more minutes down the road, we come to the left turn. Jake takes it. If I thought the original road was a back road, this one redefines the concept of back road. It's not wide enough for two cars. It's heavily treed, a forest.

"Down here," says Jake. "I remember this now."

"You didn't go to this school, though, did you? It's far from your house."

"I was never a student here. But I've driven down here before."

The road is narrow and snakes back and forth. I can see only what the headlights allow. The trees have given way to fields. The visibility is still almost zero. I put the back of my hand on my window. The glass is cold.

"How far along is it, exactly?"

"I don't think much farther. I can't remember."

I'm wondering why we are doing this. Why don't we just leave the drinks to melt? I would rather get home and clean up myself than spend however long driving deeper into these fields. Nothing makes sense. I want this to end.

"I bet it's nice during the day," I say. "Peaceful." Trying to be positive.

"Yeah, definitely remote."

"How's the road?"

"Messy, slick; I'm going slow. It hasn't been plowed yet. It shouldn't be much farther. Sorry, I thought it was closer."

I'm starting to feel anxious. Not really. A bit. It's been a long night. The drive there, the walk around the farm, meeting his parents. His mom. What his dad said. His brother. And thinking about ending things this entire time. Everything. And now this detour.

"Look," he says, "I knew it. Up there. I knew it. You see? That's it."

A few hundred yards ahead, on the right, is a large building. I can't make out much beyond that.

Finally. After this, maybe we can get home.

HE WAS RIGHT IN THE end; I'm glad to see this school. It's massive. There must be two thousand students who attend every day. It's one of those big, old, rural high schools. I have no idea, obviously, what the student body is, but it's got to be huge. And down such a long, narrow road.

"You didn't think it would look like this, did you?" he says.

I'm not sure what I was expecting. Not this.

"What's a school doing out here in the middle of nowhere?"

"There'll be somewhere to get rid of these cups." Jake slows the car as we pull up in front and drive by.

"There," I say. "Right there."

There's a bike rack with a single-gear bike locked up and a green garbage bin up in front of a bank of windows.

"Precisely," he says. " 'Kay, I'll be right back."

He grabs both cups in one hand, using his thumb and index finger as pincers. He knees open his door, gets out, and swings it shut with a loud thud. He leaves the car running.

I watch Jake walk past the bike rack toward the garbage can. That pigeon-toed walk, stooped shoulders, head bent. If I saw him for the first time right now, I'd assume his hunch was because of the cold, the snow. But that's just him. I *know* his walk, his posture. I recognize it. It's a lope, indelicately long, slow strides. Put him and a few others on treadmills and show me their legs and feet. I could pick him out of a police lineup based only on his walk.

I look through the windshield at the wipers. They make this motorized friction sound. They're too tight on the glass. Jake's holding the cups in one hand. He has the lid of the garbage can in his other hand. He's looking into the bin. Come on, hurry up, throw them out.

He's just standing there. What's he doing?

He looks back at the car, at me. He shrugs. He puts the top back on the garbage and walks straight ahead, away from the car. Where's he going? He stops at the corner of the school for a moment, then continues right, out of sight around the side of the school. He still has the cups.

Why didn't he throw them out?

It's dark. There are no streetlights. I guess there haven't been since we turned onto this back road. I hadn't really noticed. The

only light is a single yellow flood from the school's roof. Jake had mentioned how dark it is in the country. I was less aware of it at the farm. Here it's definitely dark.

Where is he going? I lean over to my left and flip the headlights off. The lot in front of me disappears. Only a lone light for the entire school yard. So much darkness, so much space. The snow is getting really heavy.

I haven't spent much time outside of any school at night, let alone such a rural one in the middle of nowhere. Who actually goes to this school? Must be farmers' kids. They must be bussed in. But there are no houses around. There's nothing here. One road, trees, and fields and fields.

I remember once I had to go back to my high school late at night. I was sometimes there during the first hour or so after school for events or meetings. That never felt much different from normal school hours. But once I returned after supper, when everyone was gone, when it was dark. No teachers. No students. I'd forgotten something, but I can't remember what it was.

I was surprised the front door was open. At first I'd knocked on the double doors, assuming they were locked. It seemed weird to knock on the school doors, but I tried anyhow. Then I grabbed the handle, and it was open. I slipped inside. It was so quiet and deserted and the very opposite of what school was normally like. I'd never been alone in school.

My locker was at the other side of the school, so I had to walk along the empty halls. I came up to my English classroom. I was going to walk right by, but stopped at the door. All the chairs were

up on the desks. The garbage cans were out in the hall, near me. A custodian was in there, cleaning up. I knew I wasn't supposed to be in there, but lingered anyway. For a moment, I watched him.

He had glasses and shaggy hair. He was sweeping. He wasn't moving fast. He was taking his time. I'd never considered before how our classrooms were perpetually tidy. We came in every day for our lesson, occupied the room, and then left for home, leaving our mess behind. The next day, we'd arrive and the classroom was clean. We'd mess it up again. And the next day, all traces of our mess were gone. I didn't even notice. None of us did. I would have noticed only if the mess had not been cleaned.

The custodian was playing a tape on a ghetto-blaster thing. It wasn't music but a story, like a book on tape. It was cranked up so loud. A single voice. A narrator. The custodian was meticulous in his work. He didn't see me.

THOSE GIRLS. THE ONES FROM the Dairy Queen. They are probably students at this school. Seems like a long way for them to come. But back where the Dairy Queen was must be the closest town. I flip the headlights back on. Where is Jake? What's he doing?

I open my door. It's snowing harder for sure, hard enough to land, melt, and wet the inside of the door. I lean out, squinting into the darkness.

"Jake? What are you doing? Come on."

No answer. I hold the door open for several seconds, face in the wind, listening.

"Jake, let's go!"

Nothing.

I close the door. I have no idea where I am. I don't think I could point out my location on a map. I know I couldn't. This place probably isn't on a map. And Jake has left me. I'm alone now. By myself. In this car. I haven't seen a single vehicle pass, not that I've been paying attention. But clearly no cars come down this road, not at night. I can't remember the last time I was sitting in a car in an unknown place. I lean over to honk the horn, once, twice. A third, long, aggressive honk. I should have been in bed hours ago.

Nowhere. This is nowhere. This isn't a city or town. This is fields, trees, snow, wind, sky, but it isn't anything. What would those girls at the Dairy Queen think if they saw us here? The one with the rash on her arm. The raised bumps. She would wonder why we'd stopped here at this time of night, why we were at her high school. I felt for that girl. I would have liked to talk to her more. Why did she say that to me? Why was she scared? Maybe I could have helped her. Maybe I should have done something.

I imagine school isn't a nice place for her. It's probably lonely. I bet she doesn't like being here. She's smart and capable, but for various reasons prefers leaving school to arriving. School should be a place she likes, where she feels welcome. I bet it's not. That's just my feeling. Maybe I'm reading into things.

I open the glove box. It's full. Not with the usual maps and documents. Balled-up Kleenex. Are they used? Or just balled up?

There are lots of them. One has something red on it. Spots of blood? I move the Kleenex around. There's a pencil in here, too. A notepad. Under the notepad are some photographs, and a couple of discarded candy wrappers.

"What are you doing?"

He's leaning into the car, about to sit, red-faced, snow on his shoulders and head.

"Jake! Jesus, you scared me." I shut the glove box. "What were you doing out there for so long? Where'd you go?"

"I was getting rid of the cups."

"Come on," I say. "Get in, quick. Let's go."

He closes his door, then reaches across me and opens the glove box. He looks in, and then shuts it again. The snow on him is melting. His bangs are messy and stuck to his forehead. His glasses fog up from the warmth of the car. He is pretty handsome, especially with red cheeks.

"Why didn't you just throw the cups out in that garbage can? You were right there. I saw you."

"It wasn't a garbage can. What were you looking for in the glove box?"

"Nothing. I wasn't looking. I was waiting for you. What do you mean it wasn't a garbage can?"

"It's filled with road salt. For when it's icy. I figured there was probably a Dumpster back there," he says, removing his glasses. It takes him a few tries to find a piece of satisfactory shirt, under his coat, to dry and defog his glasses. I've seen him do this before, dry his glasses on his shirt.

"And then there it was. The Dumpster. But I went a little farther. It's a huge field back there. It just seems to keep going on and on forever. I couldn't see anything beyond it."

"I don't like it here," I say. "I had no clue what you were doing. You must be freezing. Why is there such a big school out in the middle of nowhere, anyway, with no houses around? You need to have houses and people and kids if you're gonna have a school."

"This school's old. It's been here forever. That's why it's in such rough shape. Every farm kid in a forty-mile radius goes here."

"Or did."

"What do you mean?"

"We don't know whether it's still open, do we? Maybe this school is closed and hasn't been torn down yet. You just said it's in crap condition. I don't know. It feels empty here. Void."

"It might just be closed for the holidays. That could be. Have schools started up again?"

"I don't know. I'm just saying it's the feeling I get."

"Why would they have road salt in the bin if the school wasn't operational?"

This is true. I can't explain it.

"It's very humid in here," Jake says. He's using the bottom of his shirt to dry his face now, still holding his glasses in one hand. "There was a truck back there. So, sadly, your theory that the school is derelict and void of life is bunk."

He's the only guy I know who uses the word *sadly* in conversation like he just did. And *bunk*.

"Back where?"

"Back behind the school. Where I found the Dumpster. There's a black truck."

"Really?"

"Yeah, a rusty old black pickup."

"Maybe it's abandoned. If it's a beater, behind an old shitty school way out in the middle of nowhere, this would be an ideal place to trash it. Maybe the best place."

Jake looks at me. He's thinking. I've seen this expression before. Seeing these mannerisms of his that I know, that I like, am attracted to, it's endearing and comforting. It makes me glad he's here. He puts his glasses back on.

"The exhaust was dripping."

"So?"

"So, the truck has been driven. Condensation from the exhaust pipe means the engine was running recently. It hasn't just been sitting there. I think there were tracks in the snow, too, maybe. But definitely exhaust drips."

I'm not sure what to say. I'm losing interest. Fast. "What does that mean anyway, a truck?"

"*Means* someone's in there," he says. "Like a worker, maybe, I don't know, something like that. Someone's in the school, that's all."

I wait for a while before I speak. Jake's tense, I can tell. I don't know why.

"No, it could be anything. Could be—"

"No," he snaps. "That's what it is. Someone is in there. Someone who wouldn't be here if he didn't have to be. If he could be somewhere else, anywhere else, that's where he'd be."

"Okay, I'm just saying. I don't know. Maybe there was a car pool and a vehicle was left behind. Or something."

"He's in there alone, working. A janitor. Cleaning up after all those kids. That's what he does all night while everyone sleeps. Clogged toilets. Garbage bags. Wasted food. Teenage boys piss on a bathroom floor for fun. Think about it."

I look away from Jake, out my window to the school. It must be hard to keep this big building clean. After all those students have spent a day in there, it would be in shambles. Especially the bathrooms and cafeteria. And then it's up to one person to clean the whole thing? In just a few hours? "Anyway, who cares, let's just go. We're already late as is. You have to work tomorrow."

And my head. It's starting to throb again. For the first time since we've left Dairy Queen, Jake removes the key from the ignition and pockets it. I forgot we were still idling. Sometimes you don't notice sound until it's gone. "What's the rush all of a sudden? It's not even midnight."

"What?"

"It's not that late. And with the snow. We're already out here. It's kinda nice and private. Let's just wait for a bit."

I don't want to get into an argument. Not now, not here. Not when I've made my decision about Jake, about us. I turn away again and look out my window. How did I end up in this situation? I laugh out loud.

"What?" he asks.

"Nothing, it's just . . ."

"Just what?"

"Really, it's nothing. I was thinking about something funny that happened at work."

He looks at me like he can't believe I could tell such an obvious lie.

"What did you think of the farm? Of my parents?"

Now he asks me? After all this time? I hesitate. "It was fun to see where you grew up. I told you that."

"Did you think it would be like that? Was it how you pictured it?"

"I don't know what I thought. I haven't spent much time in the country, or on a farm. I didn't really have an idea of what it would be like. It was about what I thought, I guess, sure."

"Did it surprise you?"

I shift in my seat, to the left, toward Jake. Strange questions. Out of character for Jake. Of course it was not really what I thought it would be like. "Why would you think it surprised me? Why?"

"I'm just curious what you thought. Did it seem like a nice place to grow up?"

"Your parents were sweet. It was kind of them to invite me. I liked your dad's glasses string. He has an old-timey appeal to him. He invited us to stay over."

"He did?"

"Yeah. He said he'd make coffee."

"Did they seem happy to you?"

"Your folks?"

"Yeah, I'm curious. I've been wondering about them lately.

How happy they are. They've been under stress. I worry about them."

"They seemed fine. Your mom is having a tough time, but your dad is supportive."

Were they happy? I'm not sure. His parents didn't seem explicitly unhappy. There was that argument, the stuff I overheard. The vague bickering after dinner. It's hard to say what happy is. Something did seem a little off. Maybe it had to do with Jake's brother. I don't know. As he said, they seemed to be under stress.

A hand touches my leg. "I'm glad you came."

"Me, too," I say.

"Really, it means a lot. I've been wanting you to see that place for a long time."

He leans in and kisses my neck. I'm not expecting it. I feel my body tense and brace against the seat. He moves closer, pulling me in. His hand is up my shirt, over my bra, back down. It moves over my bare stomach, my side, my lower back.

His left hand strokes my face, my cheek. His hand is around to the back of my head, brushing hair behind my ear. My head falls against the headrest. He kisses my earlobe, behind my ear.

"Jake," I say.

Jake pushes my coat aside and pulls my shirt up. We pause as the shirt blocks us. He rips it the rest of the way over my head and lets the shirt drop at my feet. He feels good. His hands. His face. I shouldn't do this. Not when I'm thinking of ending things. But he feels good right now. He does.

He's kissing near my bare shoulder, where my neck and shoulder meet.

Maybe it's too soon to know. It doesn't matter. God. I just want him to keep doing what he's doing. I want to kiss him.

"Steph," he whispers.

I stop. "What?"

He moans, kissing my neck.

"What did you say?"

"Nothing."

Did he call me Steph? Did he? I lean my head back as he starts kissing my chest. I close my eyes.

"What the fuck!" he says.

Jake tenses, recoils, and then leans over me again, shielding me. A shudder runs through me. He rubs his hand on the window, clearing some condensation away.

"What the fuck!" he says again, louder.

"What?" I'm reaching now for my shirt on the floor. "What's wrong?"

"Shit," he says, still leaning across me. "Like I said, there's someone in the school. Sit up. Quick. Put your shirt on. Hurry up."

"What?"

"I don't want to startle you. Just sit up. He can see us. He was looking."

"Jake? What are you talking about?"

"He was staring at us."

I feel unease, a pit in my stomach.

"I can't find my shirt. It's down here on the floor somewhere."

"When I looked up, over your shoulder. I saw someone. It was a man."

"A man?"

"A man. He was standing at that window, there, and he wasn't moving or anything, just staring, right at the car, at us. He could see us."

"This is creeping me out, Jake. I don't like this. Why was he looking at us?"

"I don't know, but it's not right."

Jake is rattled, upset.

"Are you sure there was someone there? I can't see anyone."

I turn in my seat toward the school. I'm trying to stay calm. I don't want to upset him further. I see the windows he's talking about. But there's no one. Nothing. If someone had been there, they could have seen us, easily.

"I'm positive. I saw him. He was . . . staring at us. He was enjoying watching us. It's sick."

I've found my shirt and slip it on over my head. The car is getting cold with the engine off. I need to put my coat back on.

"Relax; let's just go. Like you said, probably some bored old janitor. He probably hasn't seen anyone out here this late before. That's all."

"Relax? No, this is fucking bullshit. He wasn't concerned. He wasn't wondering if we were okay. He wasn't bored. He was staring at us."

"What do you mean?"

"He was leering. It's fucked-up."

I put both hands over my face and close my eyes. "Jake, I don't care. Let's go."

"I care. He's a fucking pervert. He was doing something. I'm sure of it. The guy's fucked up. He liked looking at us."

"How do you know?"

"I saw him. I know him. Or guys like him, I mean. He should be ashamed of himself. There was a wave or a movement of his hand, a wavelike gesture. He knows."

"Calm down. I don't think he was doing anything. How can you know for sure?"

"I can't just ignore it. I can't. I can see him."

"Jake, can we please just go? Listen, I'm asking you. Please."

"I'm going to give him shit. He can't do this."

"What? No. Forget it. Let's go. We're going."

I reach over but Jake shoves my hand, not softly. He's shaking his head. He's mad. It's his eyes. His hands are trembling.

"We're not going anywhere until I talk to him. It's not right."

I've never seen Jake like this, not even close to this. He pushes my hand away, violently. I need to calm him down.

"Jake. Come on. Look at me for a second. Jake?"

"We're not leaving until I talk to him."

I watch in disbelief as he opens his door. What's happening? What's he doing? I reach over, grab his right arm.

"Jake? It's a snowstorm! Get back in the car. Forget it. Jake. Let's go, seriously."

"Wait here."

It's a command, not a suggestion. Without looking back at me, he slams the door shut.

"What? So stupid," I say to the empty, quiet car. "God."

I watch him march around the side of the school until he's out of sight. Almost a minute goes by before I even move. What just happened?

I'm confused. I don't understand. I thought I knew Jake better, thought I could at least predict his moods and reactions. This seems entirely out of character. His voice and language. He doesn't usually swear.

I had no idea he had a temper.

I've heard about people with a short fuse, road rage and things like that. Jake just had one of those moments. There was nothing I could say or do to bring him back to his senses. He left all on his own and wasn't going to listen to me.

I don't get why he needed to talk to this guy, or yell at him, or whatever it is he's going to do. Why not just leave it? The guy saw a car out front and wondered who was in it. That's all. I'd be curious, too.

I guess I didn't realize Jake was capable of such emotion. It's actually what I've wanted, I think. He's never shown any sign of it. He's never shown extreme anything. That's why it's so weird. I should have gone with him. Or at least suggested it. That might have made him realize how stupid it was to go storming in there.

I find my jacket on the floor of the backseat and put it on.

I could have tried to relax him more. I could have made a joke or something. It just, it all happened so fast. I look toward the

school, the side where Jake went. Snow still falling. Heavy and windy. We shouldn't even be driving, not when it's like this.

I guess I can understand why it upset him. He did have my shirt off. We were going to have sex. We could have. Jake felt vulnerable. Vulnerability makes us lose our ability to think straight. But I was the one with my shirt off. And I just wanted to leave. Just drive away. That's what we should have done.

Jake saw the guy. If I'd looked up and seen a man staring at us through the school's window when we were like that, in that position, regardless of what the man was doing, maybe I would have lost my temper, too. Especially if this guy was a weird-looking man. I definitely would have been freaked out.

Who is this guy?

A night worker? A janitor, as Jake suggested? That's the only thing that makes sense, but seems outdated somehow.

What a job, night custodian. In there all alone, night after night. And especially this school. Out here in the country, no one around. Maybe he likes it, though, enjoys the solitude. He can clean the school at the pace he wants. He can just do his job. There's no one to tell him how or when to do it. As long as he gets it done. That's the way to work. He's developed a routine over all these years and can do it without even thinking. Even if there were people around, no one would notice the custodian.

It's a job I can appreciate. Not the cleaning and sweeping. But being alone, the solitude. He has to be up all night, but he doesn't have to deal with any of the students, doesn't have to see how careless they are, how messy, sloppy, and dirty. But he knows better

than anyone because he has to deal with the fallout. No one else does.

If I could work alone, I think I'd prefer it. I'm almost certain I would. No small talk, no upcoming plans to discuss. No one leaning over your desk to ask questions. You just do your work. If I could work mostly alone, and was still living alone, things would be easier. Everything would be a little more natural.

Regardless, alone in there all night, especially in such a big school. It is a creepy job. I look back at the school, dark and quiet, like inside the car.

The only book Jake has given me, and he gave it to me about a week after we met, is called *The Loser*. It's by this German author, somebody Bernhard. He's dead now, and I didn't know about the book until Jake gave it to me. Jake wrote "Another sad story" on the inside cover.

The entire book is a single-paragraph monologue. Jake underlined one section. "To exist means nothing other than we despair . . . for we don't exist, we get existed." I kept thinking about what that meant after I read it. Another sad story.

I hear an abrupt metallic clang from somewhere to my right, from the school. It startles me. I turn toward the sound. Nothing but the swirling snow. No sign of movement or light, beyond the yellow flood. I wait for another sound but it doesn't come.

Was there movement at the window? I can't tell. I definitely heard something. I'm sure I did.

The snow is everywhere. It's hard to see the road we came in on. It's only about fifty yards or so away. It's frigid in here. I in-

stinctively put my hand up in front of the vent. Jake turned the car off. Took the keys with him. He did it without thinking.

Another loud clang. And another. My heart skips ahead, beating faster, heavier. I turn and look out my window again. I don't want to look anymore. I don't like this. I want to go. I really want to go now. I want this to end. Where is Jake? What's he doing? How long has he been gone? Where are we?

I am someone who spends a lot of time alone. I cherish my solitude. Jake thinks I spend too much time alone. He might be right. But I don't want to be alone now. Not here. Like Jake and I were talking about on the drive, context is everything.

There is a fourth bang. It's the loudest yet. It's definitely coming from inside the school. This is stupid. It's Jake who has to work in the morning, not me. I can sleep in. Why did I agree to this? I shouldn't have come with him. I should have ended things long ago. How did I end up here? I shouldn't have agreed to visit his parents, to visit the house he grew up in. That wasn't fair. But I was curious. I should be home, reading, or sleeping. It wasn't the right time. I should be in bed. I knew Jake and I weren't going to last. I did. I knew from the beginning. Now I'm sitting in this stupid, freezing car. I open my door. More cold rushes in.

"JAAAAAAAKE!"

No answer. How long has it been? Ten minutes? Longer? Shouldn't he be back by now? It happened so fast. He was obsessed with confronting that man. Does that mean talking to him, or yelling or fighting or . . . ? What's the point?

It is almost like Jake is upset about something else, something

I'm not aware of. Maybe I should go in and look for him. I can't wait here in the car forever. He told me to stay here. It was the last thing he said.

I don't care if he's mad. He shouldn't have left me out here all alone. In the dark. In the cold. Thinking of ending things. It's crazy. We're in the fucking middle of fucking nowhere. This is really unfair and shitty. How long am I supposed to sit here?

But what else can I do? I don't have many other options. I have to stay. There's nowhere to walk to from here. It's too cold and dark, anyway. There's no way to call someone, because my stupid phone is dead. I have to wait. But I don't want to just sit here in the cold. It'll just keep getting colder. I have to find him.

I turn around and run my hand along the floor behind the driver's seat. I'm trying to find Jake's wool hat. I saw him put it there when we first got into the car. I feel it. It'll be a bit big for me, but I'll need it. I put it on. It's not too big. It fits better than expected.

I open the car door, swing my legs out, and stand up. I shut the door without slamming it.

I move slowly toward the school. I'm shivering. All I can hear are my feet on the pavement, crunching snow. It's a dark night. Dark. It must always be dark out here. My breath is visible but evaporates around me. The snow is falling on an angle with the wind. For a few seconds, a moment, I'm not sure how long, I look up at the sky, all the stars. It's unusual that I can see so many stars. I would have assumed the storm would bring clouds. Stars. Everywhere.

I get up to the school window and peer in. I visor my eyes with my hands. There are blinds, from floor to ceiling. I can't see anyone through the cracks. It looks like a library or an office. There are bookshelves. I knock on the cold glass. I look back at the car. I'm about thirty feet from it. I knock again, harder this time.

I see the green garbage can. I walk over to it and remove the lid. Jake was right. It's half full of beige salt. I replace the lid. It doesn't fit. It's dented and warped. I can't go sit in that car again. I have to go look for Jake. I walk toward the side of the school where Jake went. I can still make out his steps, barely.

I was expecting to find a play structure out here. But this is a high school; they wouldn't have one. I turn the corner, following Jake's path. I begged him to stay in the car with me. We don't have to be here.

I see two green Dumpsters up ahead, and beyond them, more darkness, fields. Those must be the Dumpsters where he got rid of the cups. Where is he?

"Jake!" I call, walking toward the Dumpsters. I'm feeling uneasy, skittish. I don't love it here. I don't like being here alone. "What are you doing? Jake? JAAAKE?"

I can't hear anything. The wind. On my left is a basketball court. There's no mesh or chain on the bent rims. I see soccer goalposts ahead in the field. There is no netting on them. Rusty soccer posts at either end of the field.

Why did we stop here? Did I really need confirmation to end things? I'm going to be single for a long time, probably forever, and I'm fine with that. I am. I'm happy on my own. Lonely, but

content. Being alone isn't the worst thing. It's okay to be lonely. I can deal with loneliness. We can't have everything. I can't have everything.

I see a door ahead, just beyond the Dumpsters. Jake must be in the school.

The wind is worse behind the school. It's like a wind tunnel. I have to hold the top of my jacket together. I walk steadily, head down, toward the windows by the door.

We weren't going to last. I knew it. I did. He was excited about this trip under the perception of our advancing relationship. He wouldn't have wanted me at his parents' place had he known everything I was thinking. It's so rare for others to know everything we're thinking. Even those we're closest to, or seemingly closest to. Maybe it's impossible. Maybe even in the longest, closest, most successful marriages, the one partner doesn't always know what the other is thinking. We're never inside someone else's head. We can never really know someone else's thoughts. And it's thoughts that count. Thought is reality. Actions can be faked.

I get up to the windows and look in. A long hall. I can't see all the way to the end. It's dark. I knock on the glass. I want to yell but know it won't do anything.

Something moves at the far end of the hall. Is it Jake? I don't think it is. Jake was right. Someone. Someone's in there.

I duck down, away from the window. My heart almost explodes. I peer back in. I can't hear anything. There is someone! It's a man.

A very tall figure. There's something dangling from his arm.

He's facing this way. He's not moving. I don't think he can see me. Not from so far away. Why isn't he moving? What's he doing? He's just standing there. Motionless.

It's a broom or mop that he's holding. I want to stare but am suddenly too scared. I pull my head back to the brick wall. I don't want him to see me. I close my eyes and cover my mouth with my hand. I shouldn't be here. I shouldn't. I'm breathing through my nostrils, sucking air in and pushing it out forcefully, anxiously.

I feel like I'm underwater, weighed down, helpless. I can feel my pulse jumping, jumping. Maybe he can help me. Maybe I should ask him where Jake is. I wait for twenty seconds or so and very slowly lean my head forward to get another look.

He's still there, in the same spot. Standing, looking this way. Looking at me. I want to yell out, "What have you done with Jake?" But why would I? How do I know if he's done anything to Jake? I need to keep still, quiet. I'm too scared. He's a tall, skinny figure. I can't see clearly enough. The hall is so long. He looks old, maybe stoop-shouldered. He's wearing dark-blue pants, I think. A dark shirt, too: looks like work clothes.

What's on his hands? Yellow gloves? Rubber gloves? The yellow extends halfway up his forearms. There's something on his head. I can't see his face. It's a mask. I shouldn't look. I should stay down, hidden. I should be looking for a way out of this. I'm sweating. I can feel it on my neck, my back.

He's holding the mop. He might be moving it around the floor now. I'm squinting hard. He's moving. Almost like he's dancing with the mop.

I lean back against the wall, out of sight. When I look again, he's gone. No, he's there! He's on the floor. He's lying facedown on the floor. His arms are tucked along his sides. He's just lying there. His head might be moving, from side to side. Up and down a bit, too, maybe. I don't like this. Is he crawling? He is. He's crawling, slithering down the hall, off to his right.

This isn't good. I have to find Jake. We have to get out of here. We have to leave right now. This is seriously wrong.

I run to the side door. I have to go in.

I pull the handle. It's open. I step through. The floor is tiled. The hall is very dimly lit and stretches out in front of me, endless.

"Jake?"

There's a distinct smell in here, antiseptic, chemical, cleaning products. It won't be good for my head. I'd forgotten about my headache but am reminded of it. A dull ache. Still there.

"Hello?"

I take a few steps. The door closes behind me with a heavy click.

"JAKE!"

There's a wood-and-glass display case to my left. Trophies and plaques and banners. Farther ahead, on the right, must be the main office. I walk up to the office windows and look in. It looks old, the furniture, chairs, and carpet. There are several desks.

The rest of the hall ahead of me is all lockers. Dark ones, painted blue. As I move down the hall I pass doors in between the lockers. All the doors are closed. The lights are out. There's another hall at the end of this one.

I go up to one of the doors and try it. It's locked. There's a

single, vertical rectangular window. I look in. Desks and chairs. A typical classroom. The overhead lights in the hall seem to be on a dim setting. Maybe to conserve energy. They aren't very bright in this hall.

My wet shoes squeak on the floor with each step. It would be hard to walk quietly. There's a set of open double doors at the end of the hall. I get to those, look through, right, then left.

"Jake? Hello? Is anyone here? Hello?"

Nothing.

I walk through and turn left. More lockers. Except for the pattern on the floor, which is a different design and color, this hallway is identical to the other. Down the next hallway, I see an open door. It's a wooden door, no window. But it's wide-open. I walk down the hall and take a small step inside. I knock on the open door.

"Hello?"

The first thing I see is a silver bucket with grayish water in it. There's something familiar about this room. I knew how it would look before I got here. The bucket's the kind on four wheels. And there's no mop. I think about calling for Jake again but don't.

The room—it feels more like a large closet—is mostly empty, dingy. I take a couple of steps in and see there's a calendar taped on the far wall. There's a drain in the middle of the concrete floor. It looks wet.

At the back and left of the room, against the wall, is a wooden table. I don't see a chair. Beside it is a closet. It's not elaborate, just a tall closet. It looks like a coffin standing on its end.

I walk carefully, stepping over the drain, to the back. There are

pictures on the wall, too. Photos. A dirty coffee cup on the table. One set of silverware. A plate. A white microwave on a desk. I lean in to look at the pictures. In one of the photos taped to the wall is a man and woman. A couple. Or maybe brother and sister; they look alike. The man is old. He's tall, much taller than the woman. She has straight, gray hair. They both have long faces. Neither is smiling. Neither looks happy or sad. They're stiff, expressionless. It's an odd photo to display on a wall. Someone's parents?

A few of the other photos are of a man. He doesn't seem aware that his picture is being taken, or if he does, he's reluctant. The top of his head isn't in the photo; it's cut out of the frame. In one, he's sitting at a desk and it could be this desk. He's leaning away and covering his face with his left hand. The quality isn't very good. All the pictures are blotchy. Faded. This must be him, the man Jake saw, the one I saw in the hall.

I look closer, examining his face in the photos. His eyes are sad. They're familiar. Something about his eyes.

My heartbeat has become noticeable, speeding up again. I can feel it. What was he doing before we arrived? There's no way he could have known we, or anyone, would be here. I don't know him.

In the middle of the desk, besides a few papers, is a piece of cloth, a rag, rumpled into a ball. I hadn't noticed it at first. I pick it up. It's clean and very soft, like it's been washed hundreds, thousands of times.

But no. It's not a rag at all. Once I unravel it, I see it's a little shirt, for a child. It's light blue with white polka dots. One of the

sleeves is ripped. I turn it over. There's a tiny paint stain in the middle of the spine. I drop it. I know this shirt. The polka dots, the paint stain. I recognize it. I had the same one.

This was *my* shirt. It couldn't be my shirt. But it is. When I was a kid. I'm sure of it. How did it end up in here? On the other side of the desk is a small video camera. It's attached to the back of a TV with two cables.

"Hello?" I say.

I pick up the camera. It's old but still fairly light. I look at the TV and push the power button. It's static. I want to leave. I don't like this. I want to go home.

"Hey!" I yell. "Jake!"

I carefully put the camera back down on the desk. I try the play button. The screen flickers. It's not just static anymore. I lean in toward the TV. The shot is of a room. A wall. I can hear something in the shot. I find the volume button on the TV and turn it up, loud. It's like a humming or something. And breathing. Is it breathing? It's this room. It's the room I'm standing in. I recognize the wall, the photos, and the desk. The shot moves down now, lower, to the floor.

The image starts moving, leaves out the door, travels along the hall. I can hear slow steps of the person filming, steps like rubber boots on the tile floor. The pace is methodical, deliberate.

The camera enters a large room, what appears to be the school's library. It moves purposefully, straight ahead, through rows of communal desks, stacks and shelves of books. There are windows at the back. It goes all the way to the windows. They are

long, with floor-to-ceiling horizontal blinds. The camera stops, stays very still, and continues recording.

A hand or something, just out of the frame, moves one of the blinds slightly to the left. They jingle. The camera moves up and looks through a window. Outside is a truck. That's the old pickup out back.

The shot zooms in on the truck. It draws in closer, shakier. The quality, zoomed in like this, isn't great. There's someone in the truck. Sitting in the driver's seat. It almost looks like Jake. Is that Jake? No, it can't be. But it really looks like . . .

The shot ends abruptly. Back to loud, fitful static. It startles me and I jump.

I have to get out of here. Now.

I walk back, fast, to the door I entered. I don't know who the man in here is or what's going on or where Jake is, but I need to get help. I can't be here. I'll run back toward the town; I don't care if it takes me all night. I don't care if I half freeze to death. I need to talk to someone. Maybe I can wave someone down when I get back to the main road. There have to be some cars out there, somewhere.

I've needed help since I got here.

I turn left and then right. I'm walking fast. Or trying to. I can't get going as fast as I want, as if I'm walking through wet mud. The hall is empty. No sign of Jake.

I look around me. Darkness. Nothing. I know I'm not, I can't be, but I feel alone. This school, busy and full during the day. Each locker represents a person, a life, a kid with interests and friends

and ambitions. But that doesn't mean anything right now, not a thing.

School is the place we all have to go. There is potential. School is about the future. Looking forward to something, progression, growing, maturing. It's supposed to be safe here, but it has become the opposite. It feels like a prison.

The door is at the end of the hall. I can go back to the car and hope Jake returns, or try to get back to the main road on foot. Maybe Jake is already back at the car, waiting for me. Either way, I can regroup in the car, figure something out.

I get past the main office and see something glimmer from the door. What? Is that a chain? It can't be. That's the door I just came in. It is. A metal chain on the door. And a lock.

Someone's chained the door and locked it. From the inside.

I turn and look back down the hall. If I stop moving, there's no sound. No sound in here. This is the same door I came in through. It was open. Now, he's locked it. It has to be him. I don't understand what's happening.

"Who's in here? Who's here? Hey! Jake! Please!"

Silence. I don't feel well. This isn't right.

I let my forehead fall against the door's glass. It's cold. I close my eyes. I just want to be out of here, back at my apartment, in my bed. I should never have gone with Jake.

I look out the window. The black pickup is still there. Where is he? "Jake!"

I run back down the hall, my shoes squeaking, to the windows at the front of the school. No! It can't be. The car is gone. Jake's car

isn't there. I don't understand. He wouldn't have left me here, not Jake. I turn away and run back down the same hall, back past the lockers to the door I came in, the door that's now chained.

"Who's here? Hey! What do you want?"

I see it. There's a piece of paper. It's stuck in one of the loops of the metal chain. A small, folded piece of paper. I take it, unfold it. My hands are shaking. A single line of messy handwriting:

There are more than 1,000,000 violent crimes in America every year. But what happens in this school?

I drop the paper and step away from it. A surge of deep fear and panic runs through me. He's done something to Jake. And now he's after me. I need to get away from this place. I have to stop yelling. I need to hide. I shouldn't be yelling or making noise. He'll know I'm right here, know where I am. Can he see me right now?

I need to find somewhere else to go. Not out in this open hall. A room, a desk to hide under.

I hear something. Steps. Slow. Rubber boots on the floor. The sound's coming from the other hall. I need to hide. Now.

I run away from the steps, left down the hall. I go through a set of double doors into a large room with glowing vending machines at the back and long tables, a cafeteria. There's a stage at the front of the room. There's a single door at the far side. I run past the tables and through the door.

It opens into a stairwell. I need to keep going, farther away. My only option is to go up. I need to be quiet as I climb, but there's an

echo. I'm not sure if he's following. I stop halfway up the stairs and listen. I can't hear anything. There are no windows in this stair-well. I can still smell that same smell, the chemical scent. It's even stronger in here. My head hurts.

Once I reach the landing, I'm sweating more. It's pouring off me. I unzip my jacket. There's a door to my right, or I can climb the stairs to a third floor. I try the door. It's unlocked and I go through. The door closes behind me.

Another hall of lockers and classrooms. There's a water foun-tain directly to my left. I didn't realize how thirsty I am. I bend down and take a sip. I splash some water onto my face and some around to the back of my neck. I'm out of breath. The hall up here looks very much like the one downstairs. These halls, this school, it's all just a big maze. A trap.

Music starts playing through the PA system.

It's not very loud. An old country song. I know it. "Hey, Good Lookin'." The same song that radio station was playing in the car when Jake and I were driving to the farm. The same one.

There's a long bench at the side of the hall. I get down on my knees and half lie, half crouch behind it, on my side. I'm mostly hidden here. The floor is hard. I can see if anyone comes through the door. I'm watching the door. The song plays through until the end. There is a second or two break, and then it starts up again from the beginning. I try to cover my ears but can still hear it, the same song. I'm trying, but I can't hold it in any longer. I start to cry.

*   *   *

BEFORE RIGHT NOW, BEFORE THIS, before tonight, when anyone asked me about the scariest thing that ever happened to me, I told them the same story. I told them about Ms. Veal. Most people I tell don't find this story scary. They seem bored, almost disappointed when I get to the end. My story is not like a movie, I'll say. It's not heart-stopping or intense or bloodcurdling or graphic or violent. No jump scares. To me, these qualities aren't usually scary. Something that disorients, that unsettles what's taken for granted, something that disturbs and disrupts reality—that's scary.

Maybe the Ms. Veal incident isn't scary to others because it lacks drama. It's just life. But to me, that's why it was scary. It still is.

I didn't want to go and live with Ms. Veal.

The first time I met Ms. Veal was in my kitchen. I was seven. I'd been hearing her name for years. I knew she called my mom a lot. She called my mom to tell her all the bad things that had been happening to her. Mom would always listen. It wasn't like Mom didn't have her own issues. And these calls would go on for hours at a time.

Sometimes I'd answer when she called, and as soon as I heard her voice, I felt uneasy. Sometimes I would try to listen after my mom picked up another phone, but always within a few seconds she would say, "Yes, okay. I've got it, you can hang up now."

Ms. Veal had a cast on her right hand. I remember Mom saying there was always something wrong with Ms. Veal, a tensor bandage on her wrist or a brace on her knee. Her face was the way I'd pictured her voice on the phone—sharp and old. She had curly reddish-brown hair.

She was over at our house because she was collecting our bacon fat. Mom used to keep our bacon fat in a container in the freezer. Ms. Veal made Yorkshire pudding with bacon fat but never cooked bacon herself. Every so often, Mom would meet her somewhere or go over to her house with the fat.

This one time, Mom invited Ms. Veal over. I was home sick from school and was sitting in the kitchen. Mom made tea; Ms. Veal brought her oatmeal cookies. The fat exchange took place, and then the two ladies sat and chatted over tea.

Ms. Veal never said hello to me or even looked at me. I was still in my pajamas. I had a fever. I was eating toast. I didn't want to be sitting at the table with that woman. And then, Mom left the room. I can't remember why; maybe she went to the bathroom. I was alone with her, that woman, Ms. Veal. I could barely move. Ms. Veal stopped what she was doing and looked at me.

"Are you good or are you bad?" she asked. She was playing with a strand of her hair, curling it around her finger. "If you give up, you're bad."

I didn't know what she was talking about or what to say. No adult, especially one I didn't know, had ever talked to me like that before.

"If you're good, you can have a cookie. If you're bad, then maybe you'll have to come live with me instead of living here in this house with your parents."

I was petrified. I couldn't answer her question.

"You shouldn't be so shy. You have to get over that."

Her voice was just like it had been on the phone—whiny, high-pitched, and flat. There was nothing put on, nothing friendly or gentle about her. She glared at me.

I could barely talk to a stranger at the best of times. I didn't like strangers and often felt humiliated when having to explain something or discuss even the smallest trivialities. I had trouble meeting people. I had a hard time making eye contact. I put my crust down on the plate and looked past her.

"Good," I said after a while. I felt my face blush. I didn't understand why she asked me this, and it scared me. I would get hot when I was scared or nervous. How does a person know if they are good or bad? I didn't want a cookie.

"And what am I? What does your mom tell you about me? What does she say about me?"

She smiled in a way I'd never seen before. It stretched across her face like a wound. Her fingers were shiny and greasy from handling the fat jar.

When my mom came back into the room, Ms. Veal began transferring fat from Mom's jar to her own. She gave no indication that we'd been talking.

That night, Mom had food poisoning. She was up all night, vomiting, crying. I couldn't sleep and heard the whole thing. It was her. It was Ms. Veal's cookies that made Mom sick. I know it. Mom later said it was a fluke stomach issue, but I know the truth.

Mom and I ate the same thing for dinner, and I wasn't sick. And this was no flu. Mom was fine by morning. A little dehy-

drated, but back to herself. It was food poisoning. She'd eaten a cookie. I hadn't.

We can't and don't know what others are thinking. We can't and don't know what motivations people have for doing the things they do. Ever. Not entirely. This was my terrifying, youthful epiphany. We just never really know anyone. I don't. Neither do you.

It's amazing that relationships can form and last under the constraints of never fully knowing. Never knowing for sure what the other person is thinking. Never knowing for sure who a person is. We can't do whatever we want. There are ways we have to act. There are things we have to say.

But we can think whatever we want.

Anyone can think anything. Thoughts are the only reality. It's true. I'm sure of it now. Thoughts are never faked or bluffed. This simple realization has stayed with me. It has bothered me for years and years. It still does.

"Are you good or are you bad?"

What scares me most now is that I don't know the answer.

I STAYED BEHIND THE BENCH for probably an hour. It could have been much longer. I'm not sure. How long is an hour? A minute? A year? My hip and knee went numb from the way I was positioned. I had to contort myself in an unnatural way. I've lost track of time. Of course you lose track of time when you're alone. Time always passes.

That song kept replaying: "Hey, Good Lookin'" over and over and over. Twenty or thirty or a hundred times. It might have gotten louder, too. An hour is the same as two hours. An hour is forever. It's hard to know. It's only just stopped. It stopped halfway through a verse. I hate that song. I hate the way I had to listen to it. I didn't want to listen. But now I know all the words by heart. When it stopped, it shocked me. It woke me up. I'd been lying down using Jake's hat as a pillow.

I've decided I have to keep moving. No good lying down, hiding behind this bench. I'm a target. I'm too visible here. That's the first thing Jake would tell me if he were here with me. But he's not. My knee is really sore. My head is still aching, and spinning. I almost forgot about it. It's just there. Jake would tell me to stop thinking about the pain, too.

You never think you'll be in a situation like this. Being watched, stalked, held captive, alone. You hear about these things. You read about them from time to time. You feel sick about the possibility that someone would be capable of inflicting this kind of terror on another human. What's wrong with people? Why do people do these things? Why do people end up in these situations? The possibility of evil shocks you. But you aren't the target, so it's okay. You forget about it. You move on. It's not happening to you. It happened to someone else.

Until now. I stand up, trying to ignore my fear. I creep down the hall, silently, moving away from the bench, away from the stairwell I came up. I try a few doors. Everything's locked. No

exit from this place. These halls are bleak. There's nothing on the walls, no sign of student existence. I've been down these same halls so many times. They repeat themselves, turn in upon themselves like an Escher drawing. When you think about it like this, it's almost grotesque that some people spend so much time here.

All the garbage cans I've come across are clean and empty. Fresh bags. There's no sitting waste. I look through them thinking there might be something I can use, something that might come in handy, something to help me move forward, to help me escape. They are all empty. Just empty black bags.

I've made my way to what must be the science wing. Have I been here before? I look in through the doors. Lab stations.

The doors are different in this hall. They're heavier and blue, sky blue. There's a large banner at the end of the hall, hand-painted. It's an advertisement for the winter formal. A school dance. They'll all be in here together, the students. So many of them. It's the first sign of student existence that I've seen.

Dancing the night away. Tickets are $10. What are you waiting for? the banner reads.

I think I hear rubber boots. Footsteps somewhere.

It's like I've been given a drug. I can't move. I shouldn't move. I'm incapacitated with fear. Frozen. I want to turn and scream and run, but I can't. What if it's Jake? What if he's still here, locked in like me? If he were here, that would mean I'm not alone, that I would be safe.

I can get back to the stairwell. It's just across the hall. I can get up to the third floor. Maybe Jake is there. I squeeze my eyes shut. I make fists with my hands. My heart is thumping. I hear the boots again. It's him. He's looking for me.

I exhale in a burst and feel sick. I've been in here too long.

I can feel my chest tightening. I'm going to vomit. I can't do this.

I dart into the stairwell. He hasn't seen me. I don't think. I don't know where he is. Upstairs, downstairs, over, under, somewhere else. I feel like he could be hiding, waiting, in my own shadow. I don't know.

I just don't know.

AN ART ROOM. UPSTAIRS. A different hall. A door that isn't locked. This could be anywhere. I'm not sure I've ever felt relief like I did when the door to this room opened. I close it behind me, very slowly, but don't latch it. I listen. I can't hear anything. I might be able to hide in here, at least for a while. The first thing I do is try the phone fastened to the wall, but as soon as I dial more than three digits it beeps at me. I tried dialing nine first and even 911. It's hopeless. Nothing works.

The teacher's desk at the front of the room is tidy and neat. I open the top drawer. There might be something in the desk that I can use. I quickly rummage through the drawers and find a plastic retractable X-ACTO knife. But the blade has been removed. I drop it on the ground.

I hear something in the hall. I duck down behind the desk, close my eyes. More time. There are bottles of paint and brushes and supplies lining the back and side walls. The whiteboards are wiped clean.

I wonder how long I can stay in here. How long can a person last without the essentials, with no food, no water? Staying hidden like this is too passive. I need to be active.

I check the windows. The bottom window opens, but only enough to let in a little air. If there were a ledge or something out there, maybe I would consider jumping. Maybe. I open the window the full couple of inches. The cold air feels good on my hand. I leave my hand there, feeling the breeze. I bend down and breathe in what small amount of fresh air I can.

I used to love art class. I just wasn't any good at it. I desperately wanted to be. I didn't want to be competent and successful in math only. Art was different.

High school was such a strange time for me. For some people, it's a peak. I did the work and got high marks. That wasn't an issue. But all the socializing. The parties. The attempts to fit in. That wasn't easy, even then. By the end of the day, I just wanted to get home.

I was unremarkable in the ways that matter in school. It was the worst type of oblivion, for years. I was scentless, invisible.

Adulthood. Late blooming. That's me. Or it was supposed to be. That's when it was supposed to finally get better. I'd get better then, everyone said. This is when I would start coming into my own.

I've been so careful. So self-aware. I'm confused less. I haven't been reckless. I understand myself. My own limitless potential. There is so much potential. And now this. How did I get here? It's not fair.

And Jake. It wasn't going to work out between us. It's not sustainable, but that's irrelevant now. He will be fine without me, won't he? He's coming into his own. He's going to do something big, that I know. He doesn't need this. Me. His family doesn't need this, either. They aren't my kind of people, but that doesn't matter. They've been through a lot. I probably don't know the half of it. They probably think we're back home now. They're probably sound asleep.

This is not the end. It doesn't have to be. I need to find him. And then I can back out, start again, try again. Begin at the beginning. Jake can, too.

It feels good to rest, by the window, to feel the air on my skin. I feel tired suddenly. Maybe I need to lie down. Go to sleep. Maybe even dream.

No. I can't. No sleep. No more nightmares. No.

I have to move. I'm not free yet. I leave the window open and slink to the door.

My right foot hits something. A bottle. A plastic bottle of paint, lying on the floor. I pick it up. It's half-empty. I have paint on my hands. There is paint on the outside of the bottle.

It's wet paint. Fresh paint. I can smell it. I put the bottle down on a desk.

He was here. Recently, he was right here!

My hands are red. I rub them on my pants.

I see more paint on the floor. I smear it with my toe. There's writing, in small letters:

I know what you were going to do.

A message. For me. He wanted me to come in here and see it. That's why this door was open. He led me here.

I don't know what this means.

Wait. I do. Yes, I do.

He saw Jake kissing my neck. He saw us in the car. He was at the window, watching. Is that it? He knew that we were going to do it in the car. And he didn't want us to have sex? Is that it?

There's more writing on the floor up ahead.

Just you and me now. There's only one question.

Terror fills me. Absolute terror. No one knows what it's like. Can't know. You don't know unless you've been so alone like this. Like I am. I never knew until now.

How does he know? How does he know the question? He can't know what I've been thinking. He can't. No one can ever really know what someone else is thinking.

This can't be real. The pain in my head is getting worse. I bring a trembling hand to my forehead. I am so tired. I'm not doing well. But I can't stay here. I have to keep moving, I have to hide, get away. How does he always know where I am, where I'm going? He'll be back.

I know it.

. . .

I WISH THIS WERE MORE supernatural. A ghost story, for instance. Something surreal. Something from the imagination, no matter how vile. That would be much less terrifying. If it was harder to perceive or accept, if there was more room for doubt, I would be less scared. This is too real. It's very real. A dangerous man with bad, irreversible intentions in a big, empty school. It's my own fault. I should never have come here.

It's not a nightmare. I wish it were. I wish I could just wake up. I'd give anything to be in my old bed, in my old room. I'm alone, and someone wants to hurt me or hunt me. And he's already done something to Jake, I know it.

I don't want to think about it anymore. If I can find my way to the gym, there might be an emergency door or some other way out of here. That's what I've decided. I need to get back to the road even if it's too cold out there. Maybe I won't last long. But maybe I won't last much longer here, either.

My eyes have adjusted to the darkness. You get used to the dark after a while. Not the quiet. That metallic taste in my mouth is getting worse. It's in my saliva or deeper. I don't know. My sweat feels different in here. Everything is just off.

I've been biting my nails. Chewing my nails. Eating them. I don't feel well.

I've also started losing hair. Maybe it's the stress? I put a hand up to my head and when I pull it back, there are strands of hair in between my fingers. I run my fingers through my hair now and

more comes out. Not handfuls, but close. This must be some kind of reaction. A physical side effect.

Stay quiet. Stay calm. In this hall, the bricks are painted. The ceiling is made of those large rectangular removable tiles. Could I hide up there? If I could get up there.

Keep moving. Slowly. Sweat drips along my spine. The gym is down the hall. It has to be. I remember. Do I? How could I remember that? I make out the double doors with the metal handles. That's my goal. Get there. Get there quickly, quietly.

I keep my left hand, my fingers, against the brick wall as I walk. Step after step. Carefully, cautiously, softly. If I can hear it, he can hear it. If I can, he can. If I, then he. If. Then. I. He.

I reach the doors. I look in through the tall, skinny windows. It's the gym. I grab the handle. I know these doors. They sound like a cowboy's spurs when opened and closed. Loud, cold metal.

I push just wide enough to slip in.

The climbing ropes hang. The metal rack holds orange basketballs in the corner. A strong smell. Chemical. My eyes are watering. More tears.

I can hear it. It's coming from the boys' locker room. I'm finding it harder to breathe in here.

The locker room. It's not as dark in here as in the gym. There are two overhead lights on. Now I recognize it—the sound is water running. One tap is on full blast. I can't see it yet, but I know.

I should wash my hands, get the paint off. Maybe take a drink. That cool, soothing water in my mouth and running down my

throat. I turn my hands over, looking at my palms. Streaked red. Trembling. My right thumbnail is gone.

There's an opening up ahead to my left. That's where the sound of water is coming from. I trip on something. I pick it up. A shoe. Jake's shoe. I want to yell out, to call for Jake. But I can't. I cover my mouth with a hand. I have to be quiet.

I look down and see Jake's other shoe. I pick it up. I keep walking toward the opening. I peek around the corner. No one. I bend down and look under the stalls. No legs. I'm holding a shoe in each hand. I take another step closer.

Now I can see the bank of taps. No running water. I move toward the showers.

One of the silver showerheads is on full blast. Only one. There's lots of steam. It must be hot water, very hot.

"Jake," I whisper.

I need to think, but it's so warm here, humid. Steam all around me. I need to figure out how I can get out of here. There's no point trying to figure out why he's doing this or who he is. That doesn't matter. None of it matters.

If I can somehow make it outside the school, I can run for the road. If I make it to the road, I'll run. I won't stop. My lungs will burn and my legs will be jelly and I won't stop. I promise. I won't stop. I will run as far and as fast as possible. I'll get away from here to somewhere else, anywhere else. Where things are different. Where life is possible. Where everything isn't so old.

Or maybe I could last in here alone. Maybe longer than I think. Maybe I could find new places to hide, to blend into the

walls. Maybe I could stay in here, live here. In a corner. Under a desk. In the locker rooms.

Someone is there. At the far end of the showers. The floor's slippery. Wet, steamy tiles. I have an urge to stand under the jet, the steaming water. Just to stand there. But I don't.

It's his clothes. By the last stall. I pick them up. Pants and a shirt, balled up, wet. Jake's clothes. These are Jake's clothes! I drop them. Why are his clothes in here? And where is he?

An emergency exit. I need one. Now.

Leaving the changing room, I hear the music again. The same song. From the beginning. In the locker rooms, the classrooms, the halls. The speakers are everywhere, but I can't see them. Does it ever stop? I think so, but I'm not sure anymore. Maybe the same song has been playing this whole time.

I KNOW PEOPLE TALK ABOUT the opposite of truth and the opposite of love. What is the opposite of fear? The opposites of unease and panic and regret? I'll never know why we came to this place, how I ended up confined like this, how I ended up so alone. It wasn't supposed to happen like this. Why me?

I sit down on the hard floor. There is no way out. There's no way out of this gym. No way out of this school. There never was. I want to think about nice things, but I can't. I cover my ears. I'm crying. There's no way out.

. . .

I'VE BEEN WALKING AND CRAWLING around this school forever.

I think there's a perception that fear and terror and dread are fleeting. That they hit hard and fast when they do, but they don't last. It's not true. They don't fade unless they're replaced by some other feeling. Deep fear will stay and spread if it can. You can't outrun or outsmart or subdue it. Untreated, it will only fester. Fear is a rash.

I can see myself sitting in the blue chair beside my bookshelf in my room. The lamp is on. I try to think about it, the soft light it emits. I want this to be in my mind. I'm thinking of my old shoes, the blue ones I wear only in the house, like slippers. I need to focus on something outside this school, beyond the darkness, the crippling, oppressive silence, and the song.

My room. I've spent so much time in that room, and it still exists. It's still there, even when I'm not. It's real. My room is real.

I just have to think about it. Focus on it. Then it's real.

In my room, I have books. They comfort me. I have an old brown teapot. There's a chip in the spout. I bought it at a garage sale for one dollar a long time ago. I can see the teapot sitting on my desk amid the pens, pencils, notepads, and my full shelves.

My favorite blue chair is imprinted with my body weight. My shape. I've sat in it hundreds of times, thousands. It's molded to my form, to me alone. I can go there now and sit in the quiet of my mind, where I've been before. I have a candle. I have one, only one; I've never lit it. Not once. It's a deep red, almost crimson. It's in the shape of an elephant, the white wick rising out of the animal's back.

It was a gift from my parents after I graduated high school at the top of my class.

I always thought I would light that candle one day. I never did. The more time passed, the harder it became to light. Whenever I thought an occasion might be special enough to burn the candle, it felt like I was settling. So I would wait for a better occasion. It's still there, unlit, on top of a bookcase. There was never an occasion special enough. How could that be?

—He'd been working at the school for more than thirty years. No previous incidents. Nothing in his file.

—Nothing? That's unusual, too. More than thirty years at one job. At one school.

—Lived out in an old place. I think it was originally his parents' farmhouse. They both died a long time ago, so I'm told. Everyone I talk to says he was quite gentle. He just didn't seem to know how to talk to people. Couldn't relate to them. Or didn't try. I don't think he was interested in socializing. He took lots of his breaks out in his truck. He'd just go sit in his pickup at the back of the school. That was his break.

—And what was it about his hearing?

—He had cochlear implants. His hearing had become pretty bad. He had allergies to certain foods, milk and dairy. He had a delicate constitution. He didn't like to go down to the school's boiler room in the basement. He'd always ask someone else to go if there was work to be done down there.

—Strange.

—And all those notebooks and diaries and books. Always his nose in a book. I remember seeing him in one of the science labs,

after school had ended, and he was standing there, looking at nothing. I watched him for a bit and then went into the classroom. He didn't notice me. He wasn't cleaning as he should have been. He had no reason to be in there, so I very gently asked what he was doing. There was a moment before he replied, and then he turned, calmly put a finger to his mouth, and "shhh-ed" me. I couldn't believe it.

—Very strange.

—And before I could say anything else, he said, "I don't even want to hear the clock." Then he just walked by me and left. I'd forgotten about it until all this happened.

—If he was so smart, you wonder, why was he pushing a mop for so long? Why didn't he do something else?

—You have to interact with coworkers in most jobs. You can't just sit in your truck.

—Still, a school custodian? That's what I don't understand. If he wanted to be alone, why did he work at a job where he was surrounded by people? Wouldn't that be a kind of self-torture?

—Yeah, come to think of it, I guess it probably would.

On my hands and knees, crawling along what I think is the music room. Blood drips from my nose onto the floor. I'm not in the room. I'm in a narrow hall on the outside. There are windows into the room. My head is thumping, on fire. There are many red chairs and black music stands. There is no order.

I can't get Jake's parents out of my mind. How his mom hugged me. She didn't want to let me go. She looked so poorly by the end. She was worried, scared. Not for herself. For us. Maybe she knew. I think she always knew.

I'm thinking a million thoughts. I'm feeling disoriented, confused. He asked me what I thought about them. Now I know what I think. It's not that they weren't happy but that they were stuck. Stuck together, stuck out there. There was an underlying resentfulness from each for the other. With me being there, it was best-behavior time. But they couldn't fully hide the truth. Something had upset them.

I'm thinking of childhood. Memories. I can't stop myself. These moments of childhood I haven't thought about in years or ever. I can't focus. I can't keep people straight. I'm thinking about everyone.

"We're just talking," Jake said.

"We're communicating," I replied. "We're thinking."

When I was resting and scratched the back of my head with my hand, I felt a bald spot the size of a quarter. I've pulled out more hair. Hair isn't alive. All those visible cells have already died. It's dead, lifeless, when we touch and cut and style it. We see it, touch it, clean it, care for it, but it's dead. My hands still have red on them.

Now it's my heart. I'm angry with it. The constant beating. We're wired to be unaware of it, so why am I aware of it now? Why is the beating making me angry? Because I don't have a choice. When you become aware of your heart, you want it to stop beating. You need a break from the constant rhythm, a rest. We all need a rest.

The most important things are perpetually overlooked. Until something like this. Then they are impossible to ignore. What does that say?

We're mad at these limits and needs. Human limits and fragility. You can't be only alone. Everything's both ethereal and clunky. So much to depend on, and so much to fear. So many requirements.

What's a day? A night? There's grace in doing the right thing, in making a human decision. We always have the choice. Every day. We all do. For as long as we live, we always have the choice. Everyone we meet in our life has the same choice to consider, over and over. We can try to ignore it, but there's only one question for us all.

We think the end of this hall leads back to one of the large halls with all those lockers. We've been everywhere. There's nowhere else to go. It's the same old school. The same one as always.

We can't go back upstairs again. We can't. We tried. We really tried. We did our best. How long can we suffer?

We sit here. Here. We've been here, sitting.

Of course we're uncomfortable. We have to be. I knew it. I know it. I said it myself:

I'm going to say something that will upset you now: I know what you look like. I know your feet and hands and your skin. I know your head and your hair and your heart.

You shouldn't bite your nails.

I know I shouldn't. I know that. We're sorry.

We remember now. The painting. It's still in our pocket. The painting Jake's mom gave us. The portrait of Jake that was meant to be a surprise. We'll hang it on the wall with the other pictures. We take it out of our pocket, slowly unfold it. We don't want to look, but have to. It took a long time to paint it, hours, days, years, minutes, seconds. The face is there looking at us. All of us are in there. Distorted. Blurry. Fragmented. Explicit and unmistakable. Paint on my hands.

The face is definitely mine. The man. It's recognizable in the way all self-portraits are. It's me. Jake.

Are you good? Are you?

There's grace in doing the right thing, in making a choice. Isn't there?

DANCING THE NIGHT AWAY. TICKETS ARE $10.

WHAT ARE YOU WAITING FOR?

What are you waiting for? What are you

waiting for? What are you waiting for?

What are you waiting for? What are you

waiting for? What are you waiting for?

Wᵉ've gone back to the custodian's room. It was inevitable. We understand that now. It's what we knew would happen. There was no other option. After everything, it's all there is.

We passed the woodworking and auto classrooms. We went by a door that read *Dance Studio*. There was another that read *Student Council*. We saw the drama department. We didn't try any of those doors. What's the point? We've been walking by these doors on these floors for years. After all this time, even the dust is familiar. We don't care if they're clean.

The custodian's room is ours. It's where we're meant to be. In the end, we can't deny who we are, who we were, where we've been. Who we want to be doesn't matter when there's no way to get there.

We passed the door to the basement.

This is who we are. Fingernails. Fistfuls of hair. Blood on our own hands.

We saw the photos. The man. We understand. We do. We wish it weren't true.

Whoever works here, the custodian, he's not in here. We realize it as we look at his face in the photo. He's not here anymore. He's already gone.

It's us. We're in here now. With Jake. Just us. Us all alone.

In the car. We never saw the man in the school. The custodian. Only Jake saw him. He wanted us to follow him into the school, to go looking for him. He wanted to be in here with us, with no way out.

Jake's shoes. In the locker room. *He* took them off. He took them off himself and left them in the gym. He put on the rubber boots. It was him all along. It was Jake. The man. Because he is Jake. We are. We can't hold it in any longer. The tears come. Tears again.

His brother. That story about his brother being the troubled one. We think that's made up. That's why his dad was so happy we were visiting, that we'd been kind to Jake. *He* was the troubled one. Jake. Not his brother. There is no brother. There should have been, but there wasn't. And Jake's parents? They died a long time ago, like the hair that we can see, the hair that grows on our head, the hair that falls out. It's already dead. Dead a long time ago.

Jake once told me, "Sometimes a thought is closer to truth, to reality, than an action. You can say anything, you can do anything, but you can't fake a thought."

JAKE IS BEYOND HELP NOW. He tried. Help never came.

Jake knew we were going to end it. Somehow he knew. We never told him. We were only thinking about it. But he knew. He didn't want to be alone. He couldn't face it.

The music starts again, from the beginning. Louder this time. It doesn't matter. The small closet beside the desk is empty. We

push all the empty wire hangers to one side and step in. It's hard to breathe. It will be better in here. We'll stay in here, wait. The music stops. It's quiet. Pure silence. This is where we'll stay until it's time.

It's Jake. It was Jake. We're in here together. All of us.

Movements, actions, they can mislead or disguise the truth. Actions are, by definition, acted, performed. They are abstractions. Actions are constructions.

Allegory, elaborate metaphor. We don't just understand or recognize significance and validity through experience. We accept, reject, and discern through examples.

That night, long ago, when we met at the pub. The song was playing that night. He was listening to his team chat and discuss questions but not talking at all. He was still part of it. He was engaged. He was thinking. And maybe he was enjoying himself. He was taking small sips of beer. He was sort of sniffing the back of his hand, off and on, absentmindedly, one of the ticks he developed when he concentrated on something, when he was relaxed. It was so rare to be relaxed in this kind of setting. But he'd actually made it out, away from his room, to the pub, with other people. That was difficult and significant.

And the girl.

She. He. We. Me.

She was sitting beside him. She was pretty and talkative. She laughed a lot. She was comfortable in her own skin. He desperately wanted to say hello to her. She smiled at him. For sure, it was a smile. Empirically. No question. That was real. And he smiled back. She had kind eyes.

He remembers her. She sat beside him and didn't move away. She was smart and funny. She was at ease. "You guys are doing pretty well" is what she said, and she smiled. That was the first thing she said to Jake. To us.

"You guys are doing pretty well."

He held up his beer glass. "We're helpfully fortified."

They talked a little bit more. He wrote his number on a napkin. He wanted to give it to her. He couldn't. He couldn't do it. He didn't.

It would have been nice to see her again, even just to talk, but he never did. He thought he might run into her. He hoped that kind of chance existed. It might have been easier the second time, that it might have progressed. But he didn't get that chance. It never happened. He had to make it happen. He had to think about her. Thoughts are real. He wrote about her. About them. Us.

Would anything be different if she had had his number? If she'd been able to call him? If they had talked on the phone, met again, if he'd asked her out? Would he have stayed at the lab? Would they have gone on a road trip together? Would she have kissed him? Would they have entered into a relationship, two instead of one? If things had gone well, would she have visited the house where he was raised? They could have stopped for ice cream on the way home, no matter the weather. Together. But we never did. Would any of it have made a difference? Yes. No. Maybe. It doesn't matter now. It didn't happen. The burden is not hers. She would have forgotten so soon after that first night, that single, brief meeting in the pub.

She doesn't even know we exist anymore. The onus is ours alone.

That was so long ago. Years. It was inconsequential to her and to everyone else. Except us.

So much has happened since then. With us, with Jake's parents, the girls at the Dairy Queen, Ms. Veal—but we're all here. In this school. Nowhere else. All part of the same thing. We had to try putting her with us. To see what could happen. It was her story to tell.

We hear the steps again, the boots. Slow steps, far away still. They're coming this way. They will get louder. He's taking his time. He knows we have nowhere to go. He knew all along. Now he's coming.

The steps are getting closer.

People talk about the ability to endure. To endure anything and everything, to keep going, to be strong. But you can do that only if you're not alone. That's always the infrastructure life's built on. A closeness with others. Alone it all becomes a struggle of mere endurance.

What can we do when there's no one else? When we've tried to sustain fully on our own? What do we do when we're always alone? When there's no one else, ever? What does life mean then? Does it mean anything? What is a day then? A week? A year? A lifetime? What is a lifetime? It all means something else. We have to try another way, another option. The only other option.

It's not that we can't accept and acknowledge love, and empathy, not that we can't experience it. But with whom? When there is

no one? So we come back to the decision, the question. It's the same one. In the end, it's up to us all. What do we decide to do? Continue or not. Go on? Or?

Are you good or bad? It was the wrong question. It was always the wrong question. No one can answer that. The Caller knew it from the beginning without even thinking. I knew it. I did. There's only one question, and we all needed her help to answer.

WE DECIDE NOT TO THINK about our heartbeat.

Interaction, connection, is compulsory. It's something we all need. Solitude won't sustain itself forever, until it does.

We can never be the best kisser alone.

Maybe that's how we know when a relationship is real. When someone else previously unconnected to us knows us in a way never thought or believed possible.

I hold my hand over my mouth to muffle my own sound. My hand is shaking. I don't want to feel anything. I don't want to see him. I don't want to hear anything anymore. I don't want to see. It's not nice.

I've made the decision. There's no other way. It's too late. After what has happened, for all this time, for all these years. Maybe if I'd offered her the napkin with my number at the pub. Maybe if I'd been able to call her. Maybe it wouldn't have happened like this. But I couldn't. I didn't.

He's at the door. He's just standing there. He did this. He brought us here. It was always him. It's only him.

I reach out and touch the door, waiting. Another step, closer. There's no rush.

There is a choice. We all have a choice.

What holds this together? What gives life significance? What gives it shape and depth? In the end it comes for us all. So why do we wait for it instead of making it happen? What am I waiting for?

I wish I'd done better. I wish I could have done more. I close my eyes. Tears slip out. I hear the boots, the rubber boots. Jake's boots. My boots. Out there, in here.

He stands at the door. It creaks open. We're together. Him. Me. Us. At last.

What if it doesn't get better? What if death isn't an escape? What if the maggots continue to feed and feed and feed and continue to be felt?

I hold my hands behind my back and look at him. He's wearing something on his head and face. He's still wearing the yellow rubber gloves. I want to look away, to close my eyes.

He takes a step toward me. He gets up close. Close enough that I can reach out and touch him. I can hear him breathing under the mask. I can smell him. I know what he wants. He's ready. For the end. He's ready.

Critical balance is needed in everything. Our temperature-controlled incubators in which we grow large volumes, more than

twenty liters, of yeast and E. coli *cultures that have been genetically engineered to overexpress a protein of our choosing.*

When we choose to bring the end closer, we create a new beginning.

It's all the extra mass we can't see that makes the formation of galaxies and the rotational velocities of stars around galaxies mathematically possible.

He lifts the bottom of the mask off his chin and mouth. I can see the stubble on his chin, his chapped, cracked lips. I put a hand on his shoulder. I have to concentrate to keep my hand from shaking. We're all here together now. All of us.

One day on Venus is like one hundred and fifteen Earth days. . . . It's the brightest object in the sky.

He puts a metal hanger from the closet into my hand. "I'm thinking of ending things," he says.

I straighten it out and bend it in half so both pointy ends stick in the same direction.

"I'm sorry for everything," I say. I'm sorry, I think.

"You can do this. You can help me now."

He's right. I have to. We have to help. That's why we're here.

I bring my right hand around and jam it in as hard as I can. Twice, in and out.

One more. In. Out. I slam the ends into my neck, upward, under my chin, with all my strength.

And then I fall onto my side. More blood. Something—spit, blood—bubbles from my mouth. So many small punctures. It hurts, all of it, but we feel nothing.

It's done now, and I'm sorry.

I look at my hands. One is shaking. I try to steady one with the other. I can't. I slump back into the closet. A single unit, back to one. Me. Only me. Jake. Alone again.

I decided. I had to. No more thinking. I answered the question.

—*There's one other thing I wanted to ask about: the note.*

—*What?*

—*The note. Near his body. I was told there was a note.*

—*You heard about that?*

—*Yes.*

—*It wasn't so much of a note as . . . well, it was detailed.*

—*Detailed?*

—*Some kind of diary, maybe, or story.*

—*Story?*

—*I mean, he wrote about characters, or maybe they were people he knew. But then, he's in the story, too, except he's not the one telling it. Well, maybe he is. In a way. I don't know. I'm not sure I follow it. I can't tell what's true and what's not. And yet . . .*

—*Does it explain why? Does it explain why he . . . ended things?*

—*I'm not sure. We're not really sure. Maybe.*

—*What do you mean? He either explained it or he didn't.*

—*It's just . . .*

—*What?*

—It's not that simple. I don't know. Here. Look at this.

—What is all this? This is a lot of pages. Is this what he wrote?

—Yes. You should read it. But maybe start at the end. Then circle back. First, though, I think you better sit down.

ACKNOWLEDGMENTS

Nita Pronovost. Alison Callahan. Samantha Haywood.

"Jean," "Jimmy," Stephanie Sinclair, Jennifer Bergstrom, Meagan Harris, Nina Cordes, Adria Iwasutiak, Amy Prentice, Loretta Eldridge, David Winter, Léa Antigny, Martha Sharpe, Chris Garnham, Kenny Anderton, Sjón, Metz.

Everyone at Simon & Schuster Canada, Scout Press, and Text Publishing.

My friends. My family.

Thank you.